Seniors Sizzle
Love Has No Age

Seniors Sizzle
Love Has No Age

Kusum Choppra

Published by
Renu Kaul Verma
Vitasta Publishing Pvt Ltd
4348/4C, Ansari Road, Daryaganj
New Delhi - 110 002
info@vitastapublishing.com

ISBN: 978-81-19670-75-8
© Kusum Choppra
First Edition 2024
MRP ₹250

All Rights Reserved.
This novel is entirely a work of fiction. Names, characters, events and incidents are entirely imaginary. Reference to real places, actual regions, institutions or community practices has been made in a fictitious manner. Any resemblance to actual persons, living or dead or actual events is purely coincidental. No part of this publication may be reproduced, stored in a retrieval system, or transmitted in any form, or by any means–electronic, mechanical, photocopying, recording or otherwise–without the prior permission of the publisher.

Edited by Reena Singh
Typeset by Rohit Gautam
Cover Design by Somesh Kumar Mishra
Printed by Vikas Computer and Printers, New Delhi

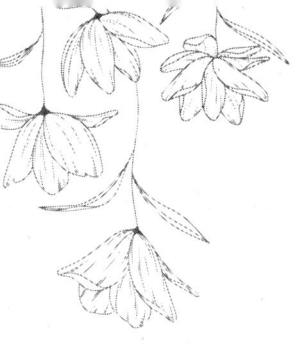

This collection of short stories is dedicated to all seniors who continue living, growing, and embracing each phase that life brings.
To those approaching seniorhood, it offers succour; a reminder that the journey ahead holds potential adventures, and wisdom too.
These stories are often testament to the resilience that seniors embody. May they inspire more seniors to embrace the challenges and the joys that seniorhood offers.

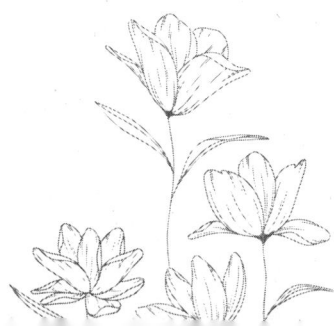

Contents

Acknowledgements ix
Embracing the Rainbows of Seniorhood xi

Accident Or Suicide? 1
Will Pipli Recall? 11
The Yellow Kurta 16
The Pink Sari 29
Que Sera Sera 38
Meow! 43
Echoes of the Soul 47
Kaushalya's Story 84
Fortune Hunters 93

Kashmir Trilogy	98
Food On The Table	113
Does Age Matter?	117
A New Dimension, Perhaps?	137
Musings: Through My Bedroom Window	139

Acknowledgements

Life teaches tough lessons; the longer it goes, the tougher they become. No guide maps exist, so we learn as we go along.

I nod in acknowledgement to Life and the invaluable teachings it's bestowed on me.

Another nod goes to all those who inspired these varied stories.

A special nod of gratitude to Ms Renu Kaul Verma and her incredible Vitasta team. Their unwavering support and hard work has brought this book to your hands. I am indebted to Ms Verma for the opportunity to be a part of her wonderful team once more.

Embracing the Rainbows of Seniorhood

Isn't it truly wonderful that seniors are finally stepping forward to claim their rightful place under the literary sun? After enriching life's tapestry with accumulated wisdom and experience, they are now moving forward to make their voices heard and stories celebrated.

This anthology is a testament to the courage, resilience, and the vibrancy of life seniors strive to grasp.

With its myriad twists and turns, Life presents them with innumerable rainbows. Each colour represents a unique opportunity to explore, learn, and grow. This anthology invites you to witness a rich tapestry of seniors from different walks of life, in varying arenas and circumstances—a testament to the enduring power of the human spirit.

It brings together a diverse cast of characters. Their stories reflect the kaleidoscope of experiences that seniorhood entails— their challenges, joys, heartaches and triumphs; vibrant hues that seniors bring to the literary landscape, with brilliant brushstrokes on the Canvas of Life.

Accident Or Suicide?

A happy sun danced its way through the room. Two men descended into the open dining room in a house as whimsical as its owner, with a series of small steps going up into the kitchen and to the upstairs bedrooms, and some going down into the basement.

'I need a break,' declared Sarita rebelliously, trotting in and out of the kitchen. The heady fragrance of both juice and filter coffee filled the air as did the sounds of toasts popping up and eggs being poached.

'Why?' demanded her hubby, Shiva sharply.

'Why not? Can't I take a holiday by myself?'

'Sarita, you've had a long holiday at home for a month, all work at a standstill, mourning your *bahu*. You still need a break? What about your son? His wife committed suicide. Yet he's been to work every single day thereafter.'

Son Sujit's fingers drummed the table.

'So? Must everyone be in step all the time?' He was treading on dangerous ground.

'You had your break when we went for the immersion. I came just to keep you safe from that deadly current. Did you know that?'

'Wish she'd carried me off!' she muttered.

'Who?' This last came with an accompanying frown.

'Ganga.'

'Who's that?'

'The river, stupid,' Sarita replied, exasperated. 'Better she grab and stifle me than live with idiots.'

'Okay, mom where are you going?'

'In search of sanity in spite of a madman and his son.'

She marched off upstairs. Father and son exchanged worried glances. Then Shiva headed for their bedroom.

Sarita was packing. Catching his baffled look, she exclaimed, 'Make yourself useful instead of standing there, simply gaping. Check out train timings.'

'North, south, east or west? And why train?'

'Better company than travelling with people with their noses up in the air.'

'Why are you going, think of Sujit. He has no one to turn to, when I go to work.'

'Then don't go to work. Be with him.'

'But he goes to work.' He sounded helpless...but wasn't really.

'Then?' she asked, giving him a meaningful glance.
He tried to pull her into his arms with a pleading smile. 'Why go?'
Her threatening look was her only response.
'WHY? Why do anything? In meetings all day! After hours, and before hours, you're on the phone, setting up meetings, dictating to your subordinates and stenos for your presentations. You are travelling for meetings all the time. Your son too. She did too. That's why, they had no kids.'

Suddenly she pounced on him, shaking him by his shoulders, shouting angrily, 'We all do these things. Tell me why?' His eyes widened at her sudden display of fury, his head bent down, his breathing shaky. He was unable to tell her the simple answer:

'Because that's how I like it.'

Everyone usually followed his lead: read only motivational books, never fiction; watch sports only on TV; spend weekends spreading 'the good word', which was his occupation, as he travelled to 'spread light'— never mind the neighbour's diyas lighting up your home at Diwali; abroad too, they travelled to 'spread light' while scrimping and saving on pennies while on a foreign 'holiday.' Wouldn't it have been better, instead, just to relax at home?

Seeing realisation hit home, she added, 'Now, can I plan my break? No board meetings, no community meetings, no internet. I just want to do nothing, except pampering my soul, maybe?'

He began to sulk. He left the room with a flourish, ordering his son to book her ticket to wherever she wanted to go. Neither father nor son bothered about when Sarita left, or from where, whether she was going to the airport or station. Neither asked; they just lived on at home and went to their respective workplaces, with stoic expressions on their faces.

Day 3

Scraping off the burnt bits off his toast, Shiva said, 'Pick up that damn phone and call your mother, Sujit. Where is she? We've not heard from her, even once.'

'Where do I call her?'

'Mobile phone. It'll ring wherever she is. She packed thermals, so it's up north somewhere...some rural or village hideout I guess from the amount of money she has drawn from the bank. Why hasn't she called?'

'Maybe no internet connection?'

'Don't be silly. If Everest can have it, why not some Kumaon mountain resort? Here, let me do it. Where the hell is Sarita holed up? She's never been out of touch before!'

Her phone remained stubbornly out of the coverage area.

'Hope she's not broken a bone trying to trek without first learning the ropes,' he commented drily.

Two days later, a call came from the hills. Police had found a body in a river and needed to confirm the identity. Was it a suicide or accident? For once, while in between travelling, both father and son cast apprehensive looks at each other.

WHEN SHIVA declined to visit the morgue, Sujit went in to get over with the identification ritual.

'Pa, we don't know if it's Mom.'

'I can't look. You go. I'm here.' His lips in his frozen face, now numb with cold, were trembling. Sujit sat down next to him on the dingy porch, rubbing the cold from his hands.

Later, he walked out hurriedly, his face drained of colour, heaving and retching into a nearby bush.

The details were sketchy. She was in a homestay, and had wandered into the nearby orchard while walking. She must have gone close to the river. No one saw anything. Shiva berated himself dramatically, saying, 'Attention seeking again?' Meanwhile, his son thought wryly, wondering why on earth had his mother gone alone and he had allowed her to do so. I should have come with her. Don't we always do everything together? Why this trip alone? he asked himself.

'Pa, she came here for a break, probably some rest from you, too,' Sujit said to his father. 'Son, soulmates don't go off on their own. They make space for each other alongside. What d'you mean, "she needed rest from me?"'

'You'd be talking about some goddamned business scheme and make her follow-up on research leads; she had been doing that all her life.'

Sujit stalked off to mull over his own woes, heading towards a little copse adjoining the cottages, where a tiny stream gurgled its way through the trees. A child gambolled there with her dog. As he drew closer, he heard her sing a familiar ditty. His stride quickened; he was listening attentively to her, now. The little girl withdrew at his approach, running swiftly out of sight with her dog.

Sujit had recognised the melody at once. 'Mom's song—should I share this with the old man?' He decided to let it be, taking a circuitous route back to the homestay. Then he settled down, making conversation with the owners.

Sympathetically, they told him about her morose mood at her arrival, and upon it improving later, when she met her little friend.

'The one with a doggie?' he asked. 'I saw her near the stream.'

'Yes, it was their favourite place to sing songs and dance together.'

'Mom dancing? I've never seen that!'

'Oh, she was so graceful in her skirt! We clapped to set the rhythm. So beautiful. She told the child stories and songs in different languages.' This was a side of his mother he'd never known. He wondered whether even Pa knew about it. But he refrained from asking him.

AS WORD spread in the village about their arrival from the city, the little one fell silent. Her mother saw apprehension on her small face and snuggled her frightened child, whispering, 'Tell Mai,' as she looked tenderly into her troubled eyes and trembling lips.

'She was like you, Mai. A...a secret between her and me.'

'Then now that she is not here —I am her. You can tell me.' Hesitantly her little secret was wormed out: she had given her a book. Relief flooded her face. A book? Maybe it was a book of stories.

FORMALITIES, FUNERAL and final rites had held them up in the rural outpost. Days stretched endlessly. Shiva trekked a lot in different directions, while Sujit kept his ear to the ground, listening to the whispers from their little pal, who constantly nattered and giggled with her dog for company.

The little girl was wary, and sometimes watched, Sujit who would often stop by to listen. One evening, petrified, she led her mother to the spot under a tree where they dug it up to unearth a book bound in a thick plastic bag. They quickly snatched it out and bundled it under a shawl. They examined it at home. It had another little something, a USB pasted inside the back cover.

Between the pages were beautiful photographs, of the lady and a young woman looking adoringly at her. After much thought, she prised out a picture, folded it carefully beneath her shawl and approached Sujit.

'Do you know her?' Sujit's double take was answer enough.

'Where did you get this from? Who gave it to you?' Her upraised hand stalled his questions. She quietly led him to the spot, and she placed the book in his hands. Back beneath the tree, he read what were not stories. Could it be described as one long story of love gone sour, into something in which love had no role? Every success meant more drudgery; habits soon overtook life, and everything was borne quietly for the sake of the son, the husband, in-laws, and society.

What expectations did society have? Parents and society expected his spouse to be a doll who never spoke, cried or wanted sex. They wanted to forsake everything that was precious to her. Numerous tiny incidents would take place daily—incidents that would drill keyholes into her heart, all of which were plugged with 'What will society say!'

'I'm used to these prickly feelings that take time to

process; is it always my fault? God, it's so tiring fighting with Shiva; it makes the insides of my stomach curl and do only I have to constantly process pent-up anger resulting from years of unspoken needs never being met? Why do I always have to fight for everything I want?'

Then came solace. Bahuji entered!

There were no dates in the diary, but there were enchanting descriptions of shared togetherness, bypassing their respective spouses. Accounts of leaving work early, practically bunking office to listen to music at home while baking fruit cakes or dancing together to old forgotten songs.

Was this pleasure a sin?

They took time off from lunch breaks to linger in trial rooms, trying on outrageous dresses in red, bright pink and purple, giggling at the thought of reactions at home. In homeware stores, they tried sitting on modern furniture, dreaming of a revamp of their up-and-down home. There was even an account of a session of them flirting in a tearoom with a stranger who was blushing pink at the randy language of two primly dressed women.

Both longed for children, but perish the thought! Their world was too ugly for the children they wished to raise!

Sujit slammed the book shut, gasping for breath, trying to absorb what he'd just read—he was shaken to the core. Mom and his Shonali were deprived of their natural happiness by him and Pa?

They only pretended—*pretended* happiness to not rock the boat? *Spreading the good word in so many places was actually selling lies that they were living!*

Before his mind wandered further, another thought cropped up:

Why did Shonali choose suicide, for no logical reason? Was she so stifled by her life, despite mom's company, but minus his? And what about mom?

Sujit was on the horns of a dilemma: dare he read more, did he want to read more of this truth somewhere else? Were there more unpalatable truths to be read? About Mom-dad's relationship? Will he be able to survive the shock of mom's true feelings, now laid bare?

Then came another new chain of thoughts.... Did these feelings go beyond mother and daughter?

Will Pipli Recall?

A pale, pensive Reshma stood up from her desk, taking in a view of the whole office. Taking a deep breath, she squared her shoulders, called for her car, and picked up her bag. This was her usual preparatory routine daily while leaving the office.

She swept out of her office, casting a scornful look at the gaggle of men in the corridor. Her glance was supercilious, as if she was almost shaming their manhood.

The driver cast several furtive looks at her pale face and tired eyes till they reached home, which was deserted at that time of the day. Reshma let herself in, locked the door and went to her room, with traces of anger, apprehension, and worry still very visible on her face.

When she stood looking out of the window, going over the whole episode, fury shook her body. Alarmed, at her own reaction, she moved to the bed. Just in time!

They found her much later, collapsed on the bed, face down—one leg hanging out, barely conscious. Bahuji was totally mystified as she struggled to turn her around so that she would lie flat on the bed, before wiping her face gently. 'Tikima, Tikima, what happened? Tell me,' she pleaded.

After briefing the elders at home, she rang up the men at the golf club before calling the family doctor.

What had happened at the office remained a mystery. No one from the office had called either. Nobody really knew what had happened. The doctor suggested that the trigger may have been some great shock.

But the evidence suggested that she had walked out of her chambers in those high-heeled shoes, quite steady on her feet, and had gone home in her car, unlocked the front door, locked it behind her before reaching her room. She had placed her bag in the cupboard and her heels in the shoe rack. If she could have done all that, then was she in shock?

Days crept into a week, then two. A routine was put into place where a live-in nurse would put her into a wheelchair, and bring her out into a corner of the drawing room facing the garden, her favourite lookout point. Later, she would help her stretch out on the new day-bed—so that she could also be a part of the family deliberations, although she lay there, mute, blank-faced.

Obviously, Reshma had suffered from some kind of shock. And soon, this was no secret. What is social media for, if not to spread the word?

ONE MORNING, the bell rang. Bahuji opened the door. A tall, round face stood there, speaking, 'I've come to meet my favourite poetess—that lady there. I'd tried to call in the morning. I left a message.'

'Who are you? No poetess lives here.'

'My name is Karnik Sharma; we often exchange poetry on the internet, before it takes shape like give it the final polish.'

'Karnik Sharma? She writes poetry?' Bahuji was stunned.

'Reshma Katyal? Very much so! She even leaves 'likes' on some of my poems, while she nags by posting harsh comments on others.'

'She's forgotten everything, even her own name. In fact, she seems to dislike it.'

'Then I'll call her by her old name,' he smiled hopefully.

'She told you?'

'It's on the Net. She said she missed it.'

'OMG!' Bahuji baulked as he strode up to the daybed with a broad smile, with outstretched hands. 'Pipli! How lovely to finally see you!'

A look of wonder crept slowly across her immobile face as her eyes turned and she looked at him in wonder. Her belligerent husband stood up and walked in from the balcony to glower at the intruder, just as a soft yet hoarse voice emanated from her, 'Is that my name?'

'Of course, it is, Pipli! Come on, Pipli, stand up and give me a welcome hug after all these years. You know me, Pipli, even if they don't,' he said, nodding at the family. He helped her up, catching her in a hug that supported her.

'And...you are...?' she managed to mumble.

'Remember that poem we tried to write together?' he asked, tapping her forehead gently with his knuckles. 'That poem to be finished together...come on, we have to go,' he urged.

She withdrew and slumped down, 'No, I cannot....'

'Pipli can. She can do anything, and everything is planned. Are you going to let me down?' The next 'No' was weaker.

'Yes, Ma, you can—you can—we'll take you—come.'

The wheelchair swiftly carried her to her room for an equally swift makeover. Meanwhile, Bahuji swiftly drew out the stranger.

'Where are we taking her?'

'Madame, I'm taking her just for a drive in the fresh air and let her recall some more, naturally.'

The hubby glowered, saying, 'Even we could have taken her for a drive.'

His eyebrows rose as he asked, 'And what will be discussed during the drive?'

The visitor turned to Bahuji, and said, 'Look. I know this is a bit of a risk, but allow me to look after her for a little while, perhaps to jog her memory a bit. Tell me quickly how it started, what triggered this?'

Meanwhile, she had been wheeled back into her room. Her breath sounded jagged and irregular.

The Yellow Kurta

Touchdown! Excited to be part of the Delhi Lit Fest, no less!

Plus, she was meeting some of her friends from Facebook! They'd never actually met. So, she was keeping her fingers crossed.

Mimi had a maverick sense of style when it came to dressing up. She barely acknowledged the 'latest' trends, preferring her own colours and styles; for her, it was all about comfort over 'latest fashion.' Her tall figure appeared doubly striking with silver waves flowing down her back as she stepped out with a big smile, scanning the name boards—there was none with her name on it.

She finally spotted a face that looked familiar, a petite woman standing next to a tall gent who had his back to the door, elbows balanced on the railing, swinging a sort of umbrella-looking contraption on his head. Staring at it, it took a moment to realise that the panels read her name, 'MIMI'.

A familiar face caught her eye and signalled to her, and a few seconds later, Aruna and she fell into each other's arms, giggling, 'I knew it was you.' They held each other at arm's length to have a good look at each other. Then, they hugged again.

'How about me?' spoke a husky-voiced gent, who was standing alongside. She looked up to a handsome bearded fellow now busy lowering the swinging contraption. 'Rajan? I should have guessed. Come, there is nothing like a hug to perk up the vibes,' she said, holding her arms open. In a split second, another figure popped up into her outstretched arms, screeching, 'Nani, I love you.' Mimi looked down, kissing the child's forehead fondly.

'*Arrey* Laddo, where did you pop up from?'

A cheerful voice pointed to her belly, 'From here, Ma....' Everyone was laughing helplessly. The loyal friends took a graceful back seat for the 'family' in Delhi. Uproarious laughter echoed right until the son-in-law appeared, perfunctorily bending to touch her feet.

The duo watched Mimi transform into a proper matriarch, offering a gentle blessing, '*Khush Raho, beta.*'

'Okay, young lady, you've met Nani; now off to school. Ma, please don't spoil her.'

'Absolutely right! Beta, off to school. I'll fix a date with you, promise.'

The friends guided her out. 'I thought your daughter lived abroad. This is ...?'

'One of my many, apart from my own, who walked through my home and heart,' smiled Mimi.

'That little one is something,' Rajan said ruefully.

'Isn't she?' grinned Mimi in response. 'Always has been. Touchwood!'

'Why? Problems?'

'*Kal kya ho kisne jaana?* Now, tell me the general plan.'

A delivery boy approached Mimi holding out an elegant bouquet. 'Madame Mimi?'

Mimi frowned at Rajan. 'You?'

He held up his hands. 'I'm here in person.'

Aruna plucked the card, which read, 'From Family. We'll see you there in the evening.'

'Hey Mimi, you have family in Delhi?'

'I forgot, honestly. I had announced the Delhi fest possibly on the family group, not realising the Delhi bunch would actually respond.... It should be fun to catch up, with most for the first time, some after almost half a century.'

'So, this is going to be your FB trip. Find time for friends, too, Madame,' Rajan added, a trifle sarcastically.

She gave him a sidelong glance and said, sombrely, 'Don't get annoyed. Can't avoid family forever. Perhaps some fences may mend.'

'But promise we'll have fun,' she said, holding up her crossed fingers.

'Like mending fences?' shot out Aruna. 'Telling family group about your visit was perhaps a wrong move. But never mind, we'll be right behind you.'

They mingled into the thick of the festival crowd, sampling the various literary wares, before settling around a table for lunch. Konica appeared to add to their merrymaking. 'What a crazy group: a horror person, a management geek, a self-help writer and'...raising her eyebrows at Mimi, 'Storyteller!' she cried out.

'So, today we'll sample that too.'

Family appeared suddenly, even as she was speaking; they waved frantically and she acknowledged them smiling, apologising to her friends, 'Sorry! Family after decades.'

The family waited patiently before engulfing Mimi, introducing themselves, most for the first time ever, all the while moving her towards a distant figure in a pale sari. The friends watched from a distance.

'Ma, see, Mimi Masi.' Mimi held out her open arms warmly and had a cheerful smile as she nodded to the sour-faced woman.

'*Arrey* Padu, still holding on to *giley-shikwe* (grudges) and spoiling your health? Come on....'

The older woman looked surprised and moved forward, hesitantly. Mimi closed the gap between them and held her close. 'Soni, look at it this way. I did you a favour; otherwise, instead of this lively family, you'd be stuck alone in Gibraltar.' The younger ones in the family doubled up with laugher till finally, a smile flitted on the dour-faced lady. She slapped Mimi's shoulder.

'You silly goose! Nobody's fault that you wore yellow and I wore blue that day. Today, again yellow on purpose, no?'

'What yellow-blue story is this? Tell us,' the family spoke together.

Settling down at an open-air eatery, Mimi looked around trying to spot her friends. They were her escape routes. Yes, all three were around. Then she smiled, recalling what had happened four decades ago.

Once upon a time, the *'Ladki Dekhna'* ritual generated great excitement; in the girl's house, elaborate dishes were prepared to impress the boy's relatives. The extended family who had numerous girls to wed had unanimously decided to centralise such events in the matriarch's house, where all visiting relatives, literally from the world over, inevitably congregated.

'These clothes won't do,' Ragini *Maami* had declared, firmly. Young Padu's Allahabad wardrobe was entirely nixed for the boy from 'foreign', who had come all the way to wed in Poona, the centre of matrimonial alliances for the community in those days. Everyone chipped in to doll-up Padu for her first *'dekhana'*.

One of her cousins, Malika, nicknamed Mimi, had made herself a new kurta, converting an old, voluminous dress into a shapely bright yellow kurta with long slits and patterned trimmings. The finishing touches on her dress made her late for her designated 'kitchen helper' duty. She floated into the gathering, heading straight for the kitchen as she walked past the guests taking a quick, sidelong look at the 'Boy.'

'*Hai Ram*, he's a chocolate boy with a baby face; he certainly will not do!'

Then looking at the array of goodies laid out in the kitchen, she observed, 'Waste of good food,' in Chinese whispers that sent the kitchen 'crew' into splits. Dutifully, she picked up a tray, and marched with it to serve the gathering. It was sampled delicately by the groom and his mother, but quickly polished off by the rest of the party. The girls exchanged conspiratorial smirks.

The guests left, promising to send word soon, implying that they had other girls to see. This was the pre-dial-up phone era of long ago. The bees hovered around their Padu, giggling, saying, 'they are a bunch of 'greedies'—don't like them—if you marry him....' The elders were surprisingly quiet, having analysed the vibes of the visiting party.

The next day, Mimi and her mother waited, but no news was announced. It was now Day Two evening, and finally, Ragini Maami turned up with a big banana split grin. Her smiles were usually rationed.

'When's the wedding?' asked Mimi's Ma.

'You tell me,' Maami responded.

'*Arrey* ask the Allahabad*wallahs*.'

'They sent word of a 'Yes'–but...' there was a strategic pause.

'But what?'

'Not for Padu...For the yellow *kurtawali*.'

'Who?'

'Arrey, that giggling girl in the yellow kurta.'

'Who was that?' her mother repeated the question. It was only when Maami looked pointedly at her, that light dawned on Mimi. Making a face, she shouted, 'They're mad!'

A hush-hush conference was held between Ma and Maami, before they entered Mimi's room. Abruptly, they said:

'Listen, he's quite a catch and looks like a hero. Has his own business. He liked you. I told them your parents will not give you any dowry. They said never mind, our son wants her, *bas*! After the engagement, we'll apply for her visa. Take her with us, post-wedding.' This last came with a flourish.

Among the Sindhi *Bhaibunds* (a premium trader community) of those times, the pinnacle of every bride's aspiration was to go abroad and live there with her husband. This was a community that traditionally had men doing business in foreign locales while the women manned the home front. Partition had changed it all, and now, a couple of decades down the line, every girl's priority was to live abroad, whichever foreign outpost her hubby was based in.

Obviously, Maami came with an arsenal of pro-wedding arguments. When Mimi's father got home that night, he listened sombrely to Maami's proposition, considering it. Then, sitting at the table for dinner, he pronounced:

'Mimi is too young. She is just halfway through college. Plus, we have older girls to marry off first. What will happen if the youngest marries first?'

Maami was well-prepared and she backed up her arguments with the following:
1. The obvious benefit of a no-dowry marriage because the boy had fallen in love.
2. He was well-settled abroad and had his own business.
3. He was prepared to wait to take her abroad with him.
4. He was not going to leave her behind for her visa to come later as had happened in so many cases, with the bride living alone for years.
5. He came from a well-to-do family, etc.

'I'll find good matches for all the other girls as well. You know you don't have to worry about such things as long as I'm there,' declared the veteran of numerous matches, grandly.

The father shook his head. 'I know you, Ragini, and also, myself and my girls. Mimi cannot go first.' Case over, he rose to wash his hands. But Maami was not defeated. As soon as he retired to his room, she concentrated on Mimi again, giving examples of happily married cousins to her.

Barely listening to Maami, Mimi, instead was deliberating on how to effectively counter her aunt.

Maami shook her shoulders roughly and said, '*Samajh*, your father has the burden of three girls. Isn't it your duty to help with a no-dowry match? One less to go!' Red-faced, she looked ready to slap Mimi, who just then, called out to her mother desperately.

'Ma, you remember where we went last week? That *kundli* (horoscope) *wala pandit*?' Her mother frowned on hearing her say that.

'What does that have to do with this, now?' Maami asked, a little angrily.

'*Ma yaad kar* (remember), the Pandit said something about my kundli? Remember…,' Mimi knew the prophecy would take on importance if it came from her mother's mouth, as she tried to recall the future for each family member. '*Ma, yaad toh kar*,' Mimi shouted, grasping her mother's hands, desperately. The noise brought her father out of his room.

'Ragini, I told you that Mimi will not be the first to marry. That's final. Don't harass her,' he said and glared at his own, bewildered wife as well. His words triggered off Ma into action. She shook her head, fingers covering her shaking lips.

'Stop, Ragini, just stop it. I will not fight against both father and daughter. Let it be.'

'But it is such an excellent match,' Maami whined.

'What's excellent about the chocolate boy whose face will never mature? After ten years, I'll look like his aunt,' sniggered Mimi, aware now that her mother had finally remembered what the Pandit had said. Had she forgotten such a vital detail just to see Mimi married off?

'Okay, tell me what the Pandit said and I'll send the refusal tomorrow morning,' Maami said, still trying to push her luck, while Ma shook her head.

'*Beta...*,' her tone pleaded with Mimi who bent down and gave her a hug before declaring triumphantly:

'The Pandit said if I got married before 24, there would be a disaster in the family. So Maami, no chocolate boy in Gibraltar for me. Let me finish college, while you look for matches for the other girls in the family.'

Maami was crestfallen, defeated as she was, by a kundli reading. She dared not suggest crosschecking with another Pandit, knowing Mimi's father would explode.

Mimi breathed in relief. She had been saved by her kundli! Otherwise, her fate would have tied her to a chocolate boy in Gibraltar. Ye Gods, what next! Maami could do anything!

No one foresaw that inadvertently, the eye-catching yellow kurta would become the cause of Padu's rejection, leading to a lifelong grudge against the wearer.

Mimi had made a place for herself next to Padu. Putting an arm around her shoulders, she said, 'Padu, it wasn't my intention to outdo you—it was just that I was itching to wear that new kurta. That's all! I rang the backdoor bell thrice, hoping to get into the kitchen, unseen. Finally, I entered from the front. I could never figure out then why you were so mad at me. Would I have spoilt your life deliberately? Look! Tell me you have had an awful life here because of that yellow kurta?' she challenged, waving her hands at the happy family surrounding them.

'Nothing happens without a purpose. I didn't steal your Gibraltar fate.... It was just not meant to be. Remember that song?' she said, braking out into a favourite Sindhi number:

Alay chhe chha mein raazi aaye, alay jey kaisan raazi aaye,...
(No one knows His will or who will please Him)

Everyone joined in merrily, adding the forgotten stanzas, clapping and humming along! Swinging happily, Mimi turned to pull Padu up. Everyone held their breath, but then Padu hugged her, affectionately. She said, 'It was pure luck that I wore blue and you, yellow. No way would I give up my Dilli *durbar* for Gibraltar.'

Then she sat down, clapping to the beat. Mimi sat next to her, happily. The younger people, demanded 'We want to hear more snippets about the family. Please, please, tell us more.'

'*Hal chariya* (crazy)! Those will be reserved for a private session. Here, let us have some fun.'

'What happened after the yellow kurta episode?'

asked another younger relative.

A giggle escaped Mimi at she recalled the story of the embroidered yellow kurta. The nostalgia of the four-decade-old story, ended with a description of Maami seething at her defeat by a Kundli! 'She ignored me for a whole month after that!' said Mimi. 'But she was a softy inside, so soon things were back to normal,' she added.

'Masi, what did you do?'

'Now? Arrey baba, haven't I had enough? Now it's your turn to do the family proud. Go on, make a difference somewhere, and let us all clap with pride.'

A voice spoke from behind her back: 'There you go, Didi, always stoking rebellion!'

She turned around to find Arjun's smiling face. 'Hey, Arjun, where did you spring from?' she said, as she was swept into a bear hug.

'It's a family tradition, didn't you know?' Arjun said to her as she spotted yet another figure from the corner of her eye, 'And so did brother dear. Bhai....' Another bear hug followed. This time, she leaned on her brother, then gazed adoringly at his quizzical eyes.

She held out both hands to her dear bhabhis, 'You know the comfort of resting one's head on the supporting chest of Big Brother. Bless both of you for making my brothers' lives so good,' she said, hugging them both, while whispering, 'I never had that comfort.'

Bhai spoke, 'Why don't you settle down?'

'With whom? Who will let me be myself—this cheery, laughing dancing me? Bhai, husbands never appreciate that, only friends can. Trouble starts soon enough with husbands and you have to pamper egos or gulp your own down. Better to stay clear. Friends come and go. Some last.'

'Friends?'

'Yes, friends. Men are always in search of fresher pastures, so best to remain just friends with them. No commitment, no hard feelings. Singles are best, single women, widows, divorcees.... We can feel and buoy each other up through pain and loneliness. That's okay and natural! No man can do that because they get stuck with their one-point agenda. Once in a long while, a rare friend or bhai like you comes along, on whose shoulder I can rest my head, take a deep breath and let it go peacefully. Where to find someone who vibes with you at this age? Better learn to live with myself and with my bunch of laughing friends. It eases the ache.'

Tears welled up in her eyes. A quick about turn, a slight stumble, then she steadied herself to take a couple of quick steps. Her loyal friends held on, Rajan with his arm around her waist and Aruna taking her hand in both of hers, to lead her away.

✯ ✯ ✯

The Pink Sari

The stocky old man entered hesitantly and stood looking through the glass panel at the still figure on the bed. He was being observed curiously by two old people, both Sunehri's colleagues. Frustration, loathing, and pleasure chased across his face as he stood for quite a while, hands clasped behind his back, feet planted firmly apart. Then he turned to sit on a chair, lost in thoughts.

'Her beauty's waned. How old would she be? Wonder if she's kept that damned sari?'

As he eased himself back in his chair for the wait, his thoughts flew back to an earlier era:

Theirs was a 'Made in Heaven' love match, despite parental reservations. His lips curled up in a tiny smile as he recalled those first three years. Gautam remembered some more, then frowned at the memory of Sunehri kissing him goodnight on the top of his forehead.

He remembered them shopping for the anniversary party. 'What a divine sari!' she had exclaimed.

'Which one?'

The salesgirl spread out the deep pink sari with a *pallu* of a lighter shade of satin.

'That's too gaudy, Sunehri!'

'Look,' she swept it over her shoulder, preening as she felt the smooth heavy silk on her arm, reveling in its feel against her skin. 'It's purrfect. Sexy feel too,' she declared, with a suggestive look.

'No, I don't like it.'

'But I like it. Can't I have what I like at least once, please?'

Adamant, she allowed him to pick another 'aunty' sari of his choice for her, but she remained fixated on buying the pink sari, too. 'I'll never go out with you when you wear it,' he said, tersely.

'Then I'll only wear it on Karva Chauth...that's a "ladies only" function.' (An annual fast that wives in northern India keep for the long life of their husbands).

The pink sari with its unique lustre and touch remained a bone of contention. Whenever he objected to her wearing the sari for an occasional outing, Sunehri chose to stay home.

On that year's Karva Chauth, Sunehri's pink sari was the focus of their meeting. 'So elegant, simple, yet Wow!'

Amidst all the chatter, her pink sari was much admired. 'So simple, yet so striking and elegant …what a find! How much did you pay for it? So smooth and enticing it feels, bet you don't feel like taking it off…!'

Sunehri had returned home in a daze, wondering whether to share all that praise with him. Lately, Gautam would turn his face away whenever Sunehri expressed an opinion or disagreed with him…. It was almost as if he wanted to control her thoughts.

But the matter of the pink sari soon went out of her hands. While she'd decided to let things be, and not let Gautam know about the wow comments it had received, he had got a call from a friend's husband, asking about the source and price of the sari in question.

Baam! He slammed down the phone and had rushed out of the house. Sunehri had waited up all night, first worried and fearful, not knowing who had called, for what, and wondered where he was. Slowly she worked herself up into a rage.

'How dare he! How could he forget he had to give me that first sip of water to break the fast? Whatever he had gone for, or wherever to, he knew the significance of Karva Chauth. It's 2 am now, and I'm still waiting,' she said aloud.

She picked up the phone to call her mother to ask how long she should wait—then decided not to disturb Ma's sleep.

Gautam came in with the milkman to find her head on the dining table, her puja *thali* within reach. She woke up to his snarl, 'Take off that god-damned sari!'

It was the last trigger, after a long night of thinking that she will make conciliatory gestures and reconcile. Unless pushed, Sunehri was a gentle biddable soul, not prone to harsh words or taking stands.

But that tone of his was the last straw.

'Where were you all night, Gautam? Did you forget it was Karva Chauth? I was starving and thirsty.'

'You should have eaten. Who stopped you? In any case, these days you do what you please,' he said, looking pointedly at her sari. That was too much for her waning patience.

'Look, Gautam, I am saying this for the last time, I am a human being with my own choices and preferences, apart from yours. I stopped wearing this sari for your sake; so why get so worked up if I wear it once for myself?'

'So you go around showing it to the whole town?'

'What town? We were barely 12 at the puja.'

'That's 12 too many. I'm going to burn it.' His eyes looked so wild that Sunehri took fright and ran into the bedroom and turned the latch. After a quick shower and change, she packed the sari away in an innocuous plastic bag at the bottom of the baby bag that contained nappies and such supplies. She was nursing her baby when Gautam hammered on the door, yelling, 'I don't have a holiday.'

Heart in mouth, babe in arms, she opened the door and deftly slid out as he walked in. She continued with her morning chores amidst some serious mental churning and thoughts. 'Have I taken it too far, this time?' she speculated.

She thought of the hundreds of times when her choices were overruled and she had to agree to purchase what Gautam wanted. Instead, all she could recall were the constant criticisms and complaints, the foremost being, 'My wife can't cook.'

Her choices, from kitchen condiments and fruits, to curtains, clothes, and even baby dresses were 'so poor' that she would leave all selections to 'Gautam the Great.' That sari had been her only indulgence in recent times.

When he left for work, Sunehri headed for her parental home with Baby in tow and the sari safely tucked away in her Baby bag. Her Pa read her face and sat her down beside him, smiling,

'*Arrey* Beta, did your fast kill your appetite?'

Amma walked in and Sunehri pulled out the sari. 'Ma, please keep this safe for me.'

The older woman gasped, 'He doesn't like this?'

As she told them about what had happened, her father said, almost dramatically.

'Am I dead that you endured such shit for so long?' His eyes welled up with tears as he said, 'Get her some food immediately.'

Gautam neither came nor called to speak to her. A

week later, some of the family troops led by a senior aunt were commissioned to tackle the crotchety Gautam. He was a tough nut to crack!

'She left home of her own free will; let her return the same way.'

'You know this is her first visit home after the baby. The custom is for in-laws to take her home with her baby.'

'I have no relatives.'

'Didn't you think of all that before making her pregnant and delivering the baby? How much did you help?' the old aunt's tone was now decidedly abrasive.

'Give it a cool thought. You have friends and bhabhis, too. We will be looking out for a party to celebrate the birth of your little one,' she added. This time, her tone was decidedly conciliatory. But it seemed all this had been in vain!

And finally, Sunehri was as adamant as her father.

'She'll not go back to that maniac. He'll be the death of my daughter and her daughter.'

The separation became a longer affair and Gautam managed a transfer.

Sunehri, meanwhile, went abroad to study and her parents brought up the little one. The family lost track of Gautam, and soon shifted to Delhi. There wasn't much contact with their old circle of friends from the old city, either.

When Sunehri finally returned to India, it was a busy

time for her, establishing herself in a brand new arena, and building a new life in a thriving city; at times she would muse over how her life had taken such a different turn. She would often muse over what her child had missed.

'Is it that easy to break up? In all these years, he has never missed his own child? And all over a pink sari?

'He hadn't liked the colour and I had loved the rich feel of that silk against my skin. For once, I was wearing the stuff queens would wear. Was he worried too many men would look at me in it?'

A bitter smile played on her lips. 'Poor man, if only he could see me now, seen by so many more than can be counted.'

Sunehri was now a professional artiste, acting, writing and producing short films; she had also spent a few years in theatre. The new medium was attractive and heady. In no time, she and two friends had set up their own little company, making short films, that immediately connected with the right audience. Her father scouted a property in NCR, as he proposed selling his old home to build a new one, with a set, edit and office space in the basement for her. For Sunehri, the bonus was seeing her daughter, Sri, flourishing in that creative space.

'Wonder what she'll ultimately do?' the family often wondered.

Busy with new adventures and raising her daughter, Sri, the years rolled by. Suddenly, Sri was about to give her final board exams. It was time to make decisions for the future. But first, it was time for the school's final bash.

And then, her heart got a sudden jolt! Sunehri paled while staring at the editing console, checking an outdoor shoot.

What was Gautam doing there? The site was R K Puram in Delhi. Quietly rewinding to recheck, she then switched off her laptop and locked herself in her little study. Everyone presumed she was busy thinking up new ideas, brainstorming by herself.

Sitting at her desk, she went into the past, thinking of her early years with Gautam.

'He's here somewhere. I saw him, clearly. He may see me, perhaps on a hoarding…what will I do if he sees Sri and approaches her? What then? Sri has never asked about her dad and I have never brought up the subject either. Why did I never tell her? Would she have asked Pa or Ma? Am I so unapproachable for my child? Has she ever asked about him?'

A new chain of thought started in her head. 'Had Ma, or maybe Pa spoken to her? But she's never asked me. Am I so career-obsessed that I forgot to address this important issue and alienated my only child?'

The self-flagellation tortured her mind and soul. When did she cry out in pain? Who was hammering at the door? Who had raced to find the extra keys, and called the ambulance?

The news spread. Her surname had changed, but the face that flashed on TV screens announcing the sudden heart attack of the talented actress, writer and screenwriter hadn't.

Suddenly the door crashed open and a young lady swept in, stopped in her tracks at the glass panel and then ran into the arms of the two old people who were waiting there.

As she flashed past him, he didn't take in the face. Images of that goddamned pink satin sari began to taunt him.

He got up and walked out.

Que Sera Sera

'To each his own. It takes all sorts to make a world, you know.' This was the gentle advise meted out by an elderly *maasi*.

'What would you suggest? What would you have done in my situation—if you were to fall out of love with your husband and fall for another man?' asked her niece.

'It is not what I would have done. I did it. Look at this rationally, dear. Parents will never be happy with a marriage to a divorcee whose divorce is yet to come through. Years ago, I did it, with greater constraints and equally rigid parents. Divorce was a sword that hung over my head, forever.'

A very wise old man advised me, 'Look dear, it is only a question of a piece of paper. A piece of paper stands between you and your happiness. So, first of all, decide whether you really feel that you want to grow old with that man? Him and no other? Decide on that first. Then, we'll go to the next step.'

There was a long pause as she thought about what he had just told her.

'Now, only you know how much you love him and want him. And his wife knows how much he loves you and wants you. They haven't been near each other for years now, but she'll not admit that and nor will she grant him a divorce. Why should she? It is a question of her prestige, her status, her pride, and her ego.

'So, it may take all of seven to ten years to get that piece of paper which will say that the Government of India hereby declares that so and so, and so and so are no longer man and wife.'

My aunt had been talking of divorce in a time long since gone. But she hadn't finished yet and continued with her treatise:

'Basically, that piece of paper, or rather, its absence is going to keep you apart more effectively than the opposition of your parents for the next ten years. By that time, you'll be going into your late thirties and he would be approaching fifty. The so-called prime of life would be over, and it would be way past your youth. You will have lost a whole decade of your life, your dreams, possibly even your chance to have healthy children of your own. For what? A piece of paper?

'You'll never be able to recreate the joys of those years, ten years on. Those will be gone forever, having slipped like sand through your fingers and into the past. For what would you have waited?

'Ten years on, your parents' objections will remain the same. They will ask the same question then, as now: "What? Are you marrying a divorcee?" They will be as adamant as ever, as they are today in asking why you want to be with a married man.'

She hadn't finished yet. 'But…but, if by then, you are already living together as man and wife, and they see that you have made a go of it and succeeded, they may begin to mellow.'

She continued: 'So, it is only you who has to decide whether you need that piece of paper to really love your Love. It is up to you.'

'And what did you do?'

'I chose to love my Love, and…to Hell with that piece of paper. When it comes, it comes. Or it may not.…

'When I look back and view my past actions, I thank God that I was too young and too naïve to see the pitfalls I was skirting. So many things could have gone wrong, but did not.

'They say God is hard on lovers. I think, on the contrary, He really looks out for us. So many things could have gone wrong.

'The day I left home. Had my father sent someone

after me, that would have been it. All my plans would have been sabotaged.

'They would have discovered the hotel where I was hiding. Fortunately, we had a backup plan and I wasn't discovered. The day we had to give up the hotel room, he arranged for me to spend a few hours until my flight, in another room occupied by a friend of his who was known to be a bit of a notorious character. I honestly didn't know about him till much later.

'I moved out of my room and just walked up to this guy's room and announced, "Look, I'm...." This so-called notorious person had causally picked up his briefcase and left, saying, "I have an appointment. Make yourself comfortable."

'Imagine, a man like him, knowing fully well that I had left home to be with my love could've taken advantage of the situation, but he was decent and he didn't.

'Then, again, when I had reached my sister-in-law's place, she could have refused to take me in. After all, it was she who had arranged the first marriage of my love, herself. But she took me in and looked after me until he arrived.

'After we got married, and he had to go away on tour, anyone could have taken advantage of me, a naïve twenty-year-old in a strange city, surrounded by strangers and no contact with home as I had burned my bridges with them.
'Anyone, the neighbours, his lusty cousins, the landlord, could have harmed me. But no one did. Instead, they all

looked after me. He could have abandoned me, rather than risk the notoriety of living with another, much younger woman and even risked losing his job and career. But he did not abandon me and nothing untoward happened.

'He came back to me and we've survived. I'll not say 'happily ever after'. It's been an adventurous lifetime, hurtling from one crisis to another, but we survived, grown old together, and bred a family. All thanks to a wise old man.

'Long before reaching your age, I had already finished giving birth to my children.

'And here you are—still hesitating? It's almost like you'll truss your parents up to bless you at your marriage much like brides used to be trussed up and brought to marry the villain in old Hindi films, remember?

'What joy will you get out of such forced blessings? For the rest of your life, they'll be looking over your shoulder ready to pick holes in your happiness. *Arrey baba*, lead your own life and be happy!

'This long wait is for what? To face later what you would have faced three, six or nine years ago?

'Que sera, sera, what will be, will be!'

★★★

Meow!

A large family gathering usually means an anniversary or birthday.

Four young couples, quite obviously siblings with their respective spouses and a platoon of kids together with three elderly women were sprinkled around the table, with kids sitting in between them. At the head of the table was an empty chair.

The conversation was lively, with lots of giggling, laughing, and teasing. Everyone's eyes were twinkling.

'Start ordering. The kids will be ravenous soon,' warned one of the older women.

Another elderly lady was conferring knowledgeably with the maître d' over wine selection, entrees and dessert. Both were loud, shushing the kids into silence to be heard.

A man spoke up:

'We're all here to enjoy ourselves. Let the kids choose what they want.'

'They have to learn what to eat at a place like this, and not always want pizza and pasta a la Pizza Hut,' came the sharp rejoinder from one of his siblings.

A hush fell when a waiter came to place an extra chair next to the empty one at the head of the table. Voices froze mid-sentence and eyebrows were raised. One voice was heard clearly above the buzz:

'Trust him to go and get himself a new wife …!'

A leonine, potbellied old man arrived, and stood surveying his family from the entrance. He walked a bit unsteadily towards them and handing something over to a waiter, he sat down heavily.

The waiter gingerly placed a large basket on the empty chair besides his. The gathering was tense, but now people slowly began to relax. A self-satisfied smirk spread on his face.

'Good evening. Are we all here? Good, then meet my new friend,' he said, majestically as he slowly lifted the cloth over the basket to reveal a pair of evil eyes set in a jet-black face. 'Meow,' the cat wailed.

A glass crashed to the floor and a chair tumbled backwards as a startled woman rose up, agitatedly. Everyone protested together.

'You know she is allergic to cats!'

'Isn't it time your Ma learnt to accept my friends? After all, how often do we meet?'

'You know she's allergic to cats. Then why?'

'What? Allergic to my baby?' The gathering exchanged glances.

The woman's son rose to escort his mother out of the restaurant.

Amidst the general pandemonium, the cat looked around, while a debate broke out at the table.

'We're leaving,' one couple said.

'No, we'll finish our meal. Besides, the kids are ravenous.'

'That'll take ages. I'll ask them for doggie bags.'

Meanwhile, the food arrived and the kids quietly tucked into their food after the waiter announced, 'No doggie packs.' The debate raged, punctuated by regular evil 'meows'.

Putting on a sorry face, the old man lamented:

'Why does she always do this? All those years together and she can't stand me now for even five minutes? Five lousy minutes?'

'You know it's that bloody cat of yours. Where is she?' A waiter finally spotted the missing pussy licking its lips after devouring a fish piece offered by another diner.

'After all these years, she wants me to accept all of hers, but she cannot accept my friend?'

'Have you ever accepted anything of hers?' demanded one of the oldies.

'But I have always loved her,' was the quick reply from the old man.

'Stop that. You have never loved her; you only cherish your memories of her at 21, when she was naïve and stupid enough to allow you to have her live in your pocket, thinking what you told her to, doing everything you expected of her, wearing what pleased you, even drinking only what you wanted her to! Over the years, she's even forgotten what she liked or wanted. And it bothers you now that she's gotten over you. She now leads her own life, without you. Now you must get used to it.'

Echoes of the Soul

Seating Uma in a secluded corner at the Club, Arun headed to the bar for his drink and a 'tall Bloody Mary in a glass, please.' He carried both drinks finding her inhaling the fragrances in the flower garden.

'Still thinking of work?' she asked.

Finger on his lips, he said, 'Enjoy this first. It's a sherbet with a spicy twang.' Parking himself on the steps beside her, he asked, 'What sort of house would you like to have?'

High on her first taste of alcohol through that tall Bloody Mary, she gestured with her arms spread out, 'A house with a big garden, flowers, a sundial, fruit trees, lots of plants and vegetables, an in-house fish pond. And, of course, hedges for bird nests.'

'That'll be filthy when nesting.'

'In that house, I could afford a gardener, no?' she replied, disdainfully.

'Kitchen?'

'Uff! Hate that. Maids must keep it clean; you inspect it from time to time.'

'Why me?' he asked.

'You like kitchens, so it's your department. Mine is books, music-dance.'

'Bathroom? Bedroom?'

'Never seen a decent bathroom. And bedrooms are for husbands. I'm not getting married. Too much responsibility.'

'I'll take care of that, then. Tell me what you want.'

Solemnly, she sat down on the lawn, thinking.

'It'll shock you.... Promise, you won't judge me?'

Shaking his head, he touched his throat, offering a promise.

'I want my father to die. He's no good for anyone. He has a vile temper and lives only to make everyone, especially Ma, miserable. Dada also suffers. For him, death will be a release. My father's death will be a release for Ma and me.'

'And your mother?' he asked, curiously.

'I'm selfish. She's unhappy, but I want her to live at least until Chhotu and Butki finish studying; I want to give her a bit of leisure time, some no-cooking days, eating out and relaxing in a restaurant, wearing nice clothes and buying what she pleases. I need her to do that.

I can't stay home, so I must work.'

Picking up the lightweight Uma, literally in his arms, he headed indoors, gesturing for a spare sofa in the club's lounge for her to rest on. A feather-light kiss on her forehead and fussy gestures to make sure she was fine, he left. The club staff was looking at the scene curiously.

Arun lingered on the tender memory of having kissed Uma on her forehead and spending time with her alone.

He rang up the office, and received a message—'Tell Arun, it is CS 4.' He smiled. This was a longstanding code from Achyut—catching up right here at four. Setting aside his notes for his upcoming presentation, he pondered:

'What is this thing called life? Was it merely succumbing to family dictats? Can I change the order of things?' He recalled his lawyer pal's lecture at the club. Ba, Bapu's second wife, was legitimate then. Today, she would have been a publicly shunned mistress trying to assume the status of Maitri Karar or second wife?

A thought struck him and he wondered about Lord Krishna's multiple 'wives'? 'What would have been their status today? There'd have been hell to pay! As it is, Ba's machinations have left me high and dry, but can't I even dream?' he thought to himself.

'Yaar, you are so engrossed that you won't even look at us? Abha, meet my friend, Arun,' said his friend, Achyut, while nudging him on his shoulder.

'So, you finally popped the question?' remarked Arun.

'And how!' Abha burst out. 'Your theatrical friend went down on his knees, dramatically demanding "Will you be my 'maitri karar'?" He's too much.' The two friends exchanged a wink.

Achyut and Abha updated him on a prospective home for themselves for which detailed alterations were being chalked out, while she weathered the parental storm that had been kicked up at home.

'Who will look after my guests?' the old man had roared.

It was now Arun's turn to share his woes, both professional and personal. Looking at Achyut, Arun revealed the growing attraction he had begun to feel for Uma.

'I don't know why and how it happened. You know me, we've seen loads of girls. I wondered whether it was because of the differences between us, but frankly, she's probably more educated than we are, in the sense of reality, philosophy and the life we take for granted. And yet she is charming and unassuming! She has no chip on her shoulders or airs of knowing more than you.

That's why I got interested in your 'Maitri Karar' or friendship contract setup. Remember, you'd explained it to me, the other day. Not bad—it's a court-registered document that takes care of the lady's interests too. And comes with a veil of social sanction.'

Achyut was startled at the mention of 'maitri karar'.[1] 'That's only for married men, Arun.'

He became sober. 'I am, one,' he said in a flat tone. Total silence greeted his statement.

'Arun, don't even try that shit. When? Where? How? Do you have any answers to those questions?'

'I have them all, Achyut. For years, I have tried to forget, but now I need to remember every detail, because it is the only way to get Uma. No one, not even Ba can raise an objection.'

Hesitatingly, he poured out an old story tucked far away in one corner of his mind. When he was 14, and on a vacation to Ba's village, he had suddenly found himself married off to her 10-year-old niece and no one had raised any objection! It had seemed like an adventure at that time, but one that had now gone horribly wrong. When she came home, she lived with his sisters. She had no time for him except when they all played together, till the time when boys were deemed 'too old to play with girls'.

---

1   Maitri karar (friendship contract) is a traditional contract system of Gujarat, now illegal, that legitimises a matrimonial-type relationship, most commonly between a married man and his unmarried mistress.

On his sixteenth birthday, he insisted he didn't want a party. He wanted to take Jinal to a movie. Before he knew it, the party had expanded to include the youngest uncle, plus a brother and sister. Jinal was in her usual long skirt, while his sisters wore lovely imported dresses. He confided in his uncle who had arranged to leave early and they stopped at a store to buy her a new dress.

Jinal did not like that at all. In the theatre, uncle tactfully placed her next to Arun. 'After the lights were off, I put my arm on her chair back with my hand on her shoulder; she pushed it off with her other hand that I had already caught in mine. She tore it away so fiercely that Jyoti told her to sit still.'

At home, she had rushed into Ba's room screeching; the old lady emerged shouting, *'Balatkar, balatkar!'* (Rape!) and slapped me and would have repeated the slap, had I not held her hand. My uncle was bewildered:

'When did this happen? I was with them all the time.'

Ultimately Bapu was called home, thrilled his son had 'grown up'. Uncle and Ba spoke out, and then Jinal was called. When she said I tried to pull her close, everyone had laughed, except Ba. The next day, her parents took her away.

'I've never seen her again. No one will tell me where she is. Finally, I put her out of my mind. After college abroad and a British internship, I started working at our mills. Hope she's not dead—that would upset my calculations.'

'What calculations?' Achyut said drily.

'Maitri Karar is only for married men. I qualify, don't I?' Arun said, wryly.

'You never mentioned this all these years?' said Achyut, hurt.

'What d'you want me to do? Boast about a non-existent wife? My touch was 'rape' for her! And now I have to resurrect that nightmare!'

'When did you last hear from her?'

'On my sixteenth birthday, and that was 28 years ago. To date, the mills have been my wife. Now, finally, I have Uma!'

'Don't be silly. It's not a game. You'll be ostracised; denied entry into family homes, events, meets, blah-blah. Abha has seen it all in the courts. She knows. Does Uma know?'

'Not yet. I have to prepare the grounds first. If the family objects, then it is just too bad. Whoever cares, will come to see us. They'll lose face when I turn up for events alone,' he said, spreading his hands, expressively.

'Tell me, can they disown me? Caste issues, social status, the jazz?'

'You can only be disowned from what your dad earned in his lifetime; the valuation of the mills in his father's time and in his times will be done and the difference would be his contribution. They cannot take away your share of your grandfather's property—that's ancestral. But it may end up becoming a lifelong battle, so don't discuss it, but keep it at the back of your mind. Has Uma said 'yes'?'

'I haven't asked her yet. First I have to prepare her for what is at stake. My people will pressurise her. What if it doesn't happen? My dreams will be shattered! I have a long way to go yet.'

'As l see it,' said the ever-practical Abha, '...first you sell the international thing to the Board with you in charge. If you're invaluable, the deal will go through.'

'Doesn't always work that way—they'll break, but not bend. So prepare for all contingencies, my friend. What if they decide to try to bring that one back? Or decide on appointing little bro, Rudra as MD? Where does that leave you? You must be prepared.'

'Your Ba will give her living hell. Have pity on the poor thing. Leave her alone,' declared Abha.

'No way! I'll convince her. I'll even go away, if need be.'

Achyut was horrified.

'Are you bonkers? Leave your family and work, for an unknown entity?'

'Help me find a way out then. You'll have to, because I need her to be with me.'

They sat down to plot and plan. Her family was the weakest link, dependent on her salary to survive and totally subservient to his.

Arun pointed to the papers on the table.

'Tonight, a roundup of our export orders and our

future plans should be ready. Everything else will happen once they agree.'

They strategised some more, with one of them wondering if he was really sure and would gel longtime....

But first things, first. Arun had to propose. Achyut insisted these plans should be made only after they had tried whether they were really compatible—physically too. 'Don't risk your luck. She's nowhere near your league,' Achyut added.

'Why don't you just tell her, Arun? As it is, she is worried stiff,' Abha fretted.

'No way. Telling her will burden her, and she will worry about my family,' Achyut cautioned. His own family had often quizzed Achyut about Arun's constant preoccupation. He had explained that it was due to work worries!

Uma herself had burst out one day, 'Sir, what is the problem? You look so troubled.' A stoic silence had followed.

'Do you think she is ready to hear what you have to tell her?' he wondered.

The next time she brought it up again at Abha's place, and Achyut had said gently, 'He's in love with a lady who doesn't realise it.'

'Then go tell her, la! Otherwise, you'll fall sick and your plans will go *phusss*. Who is she? Let me go and tell her,' she had said, to the merriment of others.

'So, my dear, can you resolve everything? Even love?' Arun had said, tears of merriment rolling down his eyes, as he put his arm around her shoulders.

The friends watched cautiously. Uma had looked at him expectantly while Arun gazed into her face quizzically.

All he had learned about Uma in this last year flashed across his mind's eye: her childishness, her wisdom, her range of knowledge, her flexibility, her background, her dedication, her integrity, her desires that were so simple, yet so great. Once she had told him, 'I wished my crippled father would die to relieve Ma's burden!'

But she was ready to work herself to the bone to ensure a brighter future for her younger brother and sister after the elder brother had abandoned them after his marriage!

One day, Arun had asked Uma whether the brother would help after his engineering degree. 'That selfish creature? Never!' she had replied.

Sure enough, brother dear had become a *Ghar Jamai* of his Surat in-laws, forgetting that the Engineering degree had been funded by his grandpa's gratuity and a loan paid from his pension, while Uma's salary was used to run the house!

Her definition of a 'proper salary' had startled Arun. 'A proper salary must allow for proper meals, decent clothes, and more than one diya for a festival and a little saving for emergencies, no?'

Finally, he put out his hands and declared, 'There

is a lady here who is so busy thinking of others that she has no time to see me, at least not as husband material. *Kya karoon?*'

'*Arrey Baba*, how will she think of you as husband material, if you don't speak to her? Is she already married?' Abha's jaw had dropped.

'If she were married, would I dream of making her mine?'

'If you can't say it here, go ahead and spell out your proposal.'

Hoots of laughter from Abha and Achyut filled the room, as Arun whispered, 'Uma, will you accept my proposal to you?'

She stood up, arms akimbo.

'You know who you are? And…?'

He stood up, holding her, his eyes blazing, 'Don't even mention that mill *malik ka beta* and mill *chawl ki chhokri* story.'

Sitting her down close to him, he took a deep breath before he said in a firm voice, 'If my sister were even a fraction of you, I'd marry her to a Prince. Uma, I see only you as my life partner.'

Achyut added, 'Uma, now he's said it, say 'yes' fast or he'll go into *banvaas.*'

'*Ulti Ramayan*,' she countered. 'I will go into banvaas, not Boss; does he even know what he's saying?'

'Uma, for months, he's thought of nothing else; he is

more than sure of what he wants. He was waiting for you to sense it; everything has been planned keeping you in mind,' Achyut told her.

Uma collapsed on the sofa. 'Sir....'

Arun said firmly, 'No more, 'Sir', Uma. You know my name. Meanwhile, Abha was addressing Uma, 'Listen, Uma, we knew before we met you. Don't you like him?'

'Didi, how can I not? He's, my hero.'

'Hero loves Uma. Does Uma love him?' the lady said with a sigh.

'This is not a movie, Didi, with heroes and heroines. It's simple for them; but in the real world? If I say "anything," before his family kills me, mine will. Then, what about Ma, Chhotu, Butki?'

'So little faith in your hero? He's prepared to walk out of his family if they don't agree. He is that serious. He has thought of so many exigency plans,' said Achyut, trying to put her at ease.

Uma's eyes sought Arun's, but his arms reached out to her and she took that crucial step into them. The other two left them alone.

The mechanics, however, could only be finalised after the two had checked whether they were compatible.

Uma's first 'work trip' was, therefore, arranged to a lush forest area with an inviting farmhouse. Abha was tasked with breaking to her what the trip was about. Shocked, then reluctantly accepting the logic, Uma agreed. The importance of this action, sunk in.

Abha asked, 'Uma, what do you say?'

'Didi, I'm nearing 30, but all this being done so clandestinely, I can see Ma and Dada (grandfather) disapproving of this.'

'Dada? How does he come into this?' gasped Abha.

'Bapu doesn't take any decisions. Seeing Ma under so much pressure, was tough for Dada too.'

'And you all knew?' Abha gasped.

'Bapu took ganja—maybe he guessed?'

That evening, when Uma headed for bed, Abha revealed what she had learned to Arun and Achyut. 'This happens at their home?'

'Why are widows isolated in so many families? *Bad Luck is just a convenient cover-up to make her available, without waking the whole household, that's it.* Her mom still looks alive, rather than becoming the dried prune that happens to so many widows. Some may have guessed, but who can bell the cat? Arun, don't even mention this to Uma.'

That night created many happy memories for both of them, as they waltzed around her inexperience and his mastery, he holding back so as to not to overwhelm her.

'Uma, are you afraid?' he asked.

He inhaled the fragrances of his woman. Whiskey worked its magic into their lovemaking well into the wee hours until they woke up to someone banging on the door.

Arun held Uma, close. 'Will you accept me? Forever?'

She nodded. 'And you?' she questioned.

'*Saat janam* (seven lives),' he said, kissing her on her eyes. The union would be well and truly seasoned by the time they headed back.

At breakfast, Abha brought up the court marriage idea, reminding Uma that she had done it herself. Achyut explained the maitri karar concept, something that had come about as a solution to various issues. In their case, it was to circumvent an unhappy, non-existent first marriage. He explained that his situation had been resolved by the friendship of the fathers of Abha, Achyut and his first wife, Kiran.

'There is always the parents' *tamasha* when a child selects a partner himself or herself. They forgive everyone when a baby comes along. Till that time, enjoy him yourself, it'll give you time for each other,' Uma added.

Then, she asked gravely, 'But why maitri karaar?'

Arun had to explain his aborted marriage!

He presented the facts. 'My Ma died. Then Bapu married Ba, had four sons and four *betis*. Bapu went astray and I was her punching bag—her *Kali Chaudas* (annual darkest day). She got me married to her niece, who ran away and I was left alone. I have since been socially boycotted by Ba, so I only talk to Bapu, uncles and my cousins. If I take you home, you'll become her target: you are delicate, refined, well-spoken, while she wants her *bahus* to be *sanskaari*, to organise all the pujas she does and be confined to the kitchen. She will stop you from going to office; and even going out alone with me will be a battle. We will have no private life, either, for Ba walks in and out of any bedroom anytime she pleases. All the aunts are like the walking dead at home. They come to life only in their parents' homes. She goes to check on them, there too.

'Uma, I will not allow you to die even before blooming. We will stay independently, where Ba will not come. I want my Uma, happy and peaceful. You are the light of my heart. NO! Ba cannot enter my home.'

'How'll we stop her?' Uma's soft voice asked. He noted the 'we.'

'She'll never come to a maitri karar place. She will be terrified that her power and sanskaars will be killed.'

Abha cut into his future plans, 'So, you want to defy Ba? What of Uma, she will be all alone in society? What if an accident happens, and then what will she do? Tell me.'

Abha continued, 'Ba being Ba, will hate Uma because she's yours. You're giving her a weapon. No wedding, only karar? Can't you hear her, talking about this to everyone?'

'That's why I need to have my own home outside the family mansion. Those who want to, will come knowing that I live with Uma. If they don't approve, they'll not come. All the Gen-next and third will come, call it curiosity or just to say, "Up Yours, Ba",' Arun added.

'But where is this first wife of yours,' Uma asked.

'No idea, Ba won't tell. Then I finally stopped asking.'

Achyut broke in, 'That's my job. I'll locate her. But for what and that too, after twenty years?'

Later, Achyut revealed he'd made contact with someone from Ba's village: that Jinal had literally gone wild at home, then had run away with a bank manager heading for an Orissa posting. Gleefully he added that they too must have had a maitri karar as the manager's papers showed him married when he'd arrived in Gujarat.

And maitri karaar was a custom known only in Gujarat.

'How can a mother do this to her own son?' Uma had said, aghast.

'Not son, stepson. Suppose Jinal had produced children like Ba did? Now, Ba's own sons can inherit more because I have no children.'

'You will lose your inheritance?' the three said, genuinely shocked.

'Not my whole inheritance. Maybe a portion; and her son will be the MD, as he has produced an heir already.'

'Uma,' he said to her, pulling her towards him, 'First understand, coming to me will entail a sacrifice for both of us; some will boycott us, others will play social politics with us and our families. Until society gets used to seeing us as a couple, the road will be hard. Think it over very carefully. Don't answer now. Take your time.'

'Can you take it, Arun?' she uttered his name unhesitatingly.

'I am only worried about you,' he said.

Her voice was pitiful. 'Won't I ever see Ma, Butki and Chhotu?' His arms folded around her, letting her tears flow into his chest.

'That time will come too, I promise.'

Later, he explained the full ramifications of their actions. It would be tough. He explained that Abha had no mother, and had only a father who was dependent on her. Her father, Achyut's and his wife Kiran's father were old chums and had ensured orderliness between Achyut's two homes. So social obligations were met, sometimes with Kiran, sometimes with Abha who also worked with him. Life had eventually settled down.

But he explained to Uma that, that would not happen in their case. Neither Ba, nor Bapu, nor her Dada would relent. Some day, perhaps, Chhotu and Butki would visit, but Ba's poison would vitiate all these plans for a long time.

'For me, it may at first, be wonderful to be free of those obligations. But after some time, we'll miss meeting up for a simple chat. Will you be able to fill your life, with just me? As children, our parents gave us miseries. This whole motherhood-fatherhood business is overrated. Sometimes, kids rant against parents, or parents at kids. Better to be just the two of us.'

His head down in her lap, Arun missed seeing the agony on Uma's face and the tears that flowed freely down her cheeks. Her hands caressed his hair.

At the upcoming Board meeting, Arun presented his possible European, American and African business connections, with projections of future profits. The members were definitely interested. He strategically did not disclose a rotation scheme in which high-quality goods would be pumped into upmarket outlets, and unsold stock rotated in other graded outlets till they hit the bottom of the market. The mills were always churning out fresh top-of-the-line stuff. It would guarantee profits with market-savvy new designs, good prices and minimal leftovers.

Arun gave his father a private rundown on the business potential of this scheme. He listened carefully, and ordered Arun to take personal charge and put together his teams for international operations and finance portfolios for the mills, and also consider other options.

The same day, Arun told them of his decision. His father pursed his lips, while Ba was at her vitriolic best. 'Wasn't once enough? You ruined my name in my *maika*. There's no place in this house for gold diggers. We'll disown you. And don't even think of getting married behind our backs. I'll make sure all the marriage registries are warned not to accept your application,' she added for good measure.

The next morning, the family men gathered in the old man's study to be briefed on Arun's choice and Ba's edict. Arun walked in with a folded sheet of paper in his hand. With a firm voice, he announced boldly, 'You don't accept my choice, so I'll not marry. These are my conditions:

'You cannot disown me from the ancestral property that belongs to me as the oldest grandson.

'The mill and other entities will remain a group that cannot be split up. They will continue to function as a group.

'My responsibilities will remain International Operations and Finances of the group.'

Pointing to his brother Rudra, he said, 'Make him MD if you want. Expansions will continue and I will function within the family group, as always. But, since you cannot accept my choice, I will set up my own establishment, not under this roof. Think all this over.'

A chorus of 'Me too's' arose around the table. The old man raised his hand, commanding silence. 'Your conditions are accepted, except for the last. We have over 100 acres here—and there is plenty of room for a house for everyone. But there will only be one main gate. That is non-negotiable.'

Uma's family was equally vitriolic in their response. Dada had declared, 'Let her die once at my hands rather than a little bit every day; being an outcast at home is too cruel a fate.' The older brother had already vanished to his Surat *sasural*, to only turn up a decade later; meanwhile, the family subsisted on Uma's 'salary', although she no longer worked at the mill. Butki lashed out at her for ruining her marriage prospects; Chhotu was, however, pleased with the prospect of a wealthy *Jija*.

The 'karar' was discreetly signed in a far-off city before they set up home together. Chhotu had warned Uma not to venture near home. He had also promised to bring Butki to visit her after a few months.

But Arun had made it a point to make regular visits to the old home, practically every other day. He would walk in unannounced, head for his room for a change of clothes, go to the library to pick up a book or magazine, then head towards the kitchen for a snack. He would look up his younger cousins who'd be overjoyed to see him, all the while, studiously avoiding Ba.

His legal guru had advised him: 'It remains your home, so maintain your regular presence there, at will.' At Navratri, he arrived after the *aarti* to join the reveling gangs, greet uncles, aunts and cousins, carefully bending for a blessing from his father, before slipping off to surface at the clubs where the handsome foursome were always welcome.

On one occasion, he had landed unannounced in the middle of one of Ba's pujas. One of the aunts approached him, whispering slyly, '*Pehli nathi avi?*' (Hasn't that 'one' come?) The answer from Arun came loud and clear, for all to hear. '*Kaki*, I don't have two or three, only one.' There was a stunned silence. Ba, looked angry.

Looking back on his life, Arun asked himself whether he had done the right thing for Uma, letting her undergo such a long punishment. Even Ram's 14 years were nothing compared to hers!

He took Uma everywhere with him, cheerfully introducing her to his friends, and colleagues from work, to his old college and abroad too. He took pride in the way she was able to merge seamlessly with all his various groups.

He relished Uma's ability to hold her own and to learn so much from every place they were in, including things that had never struck him, while they were on their foreign trips! Her mind was quick to learn and her range, staggering.

For years, Uma kept herself afloat with charities; she set up a coaching institution for kids of lower-income groups; she helped them to take competitive exams that would give them a leg up. That led her into establishing various NGOs.

She took lessons in music to enhance her own gentle voice that soon began to ring through their home. She would ask him to take her not only to cultural events, but for *garba* as well, where some of their family members would happily catch up with them. All that finally did mature into a social circle of her own.

But her soul pined for a babe in her arms; Arun had not been too encouraging.

'Wait Uma,' Abha had counselled her. 'Perhaps, he's scared of aping his father, maybe.'

'DID YOU never wonder over her sad face? Did you not ask what had happened to that old glow on her face?' Abha asked Arun, once.

He replied, woodenly, 'I always gave her the best I could.'

'That's not enough, Arun. While she was ill, did you recite poetry to her, then? Or try to find out her deepest desire? You were so immersed in your own unending campaigns that your vanity would not let you rest till the last possible knock came on your mind's door!'

'What are you talking about, Abha? What campaign of mine?'

'You really never fathomed? You're so sensitive to everyone, but yet you harden your heart to hers and still claim to love her?'

Achyut spoke up, 'Abha darling, even I've lost you. What are you trying to tell us?'

'Not you too, Achyut! Could you not see through Arun's huge passion for international business and business trips abroad?'

'He was expanding the business in so many directions, apart from the mills which are gone in any case now. Diversification was the only way to survive,' Achyut replied, even as Abha took a deep breath.

'Listen my two nut-heads. The mills were dead and diversification was the only way out. Didn't the rest of the family know that? Our man is not the MD of the group. So, whose responsibility was that? Why did he take it upon himself? Wait, first, hear me out....

'Do you men realise that Arun's mission was to make himself indispensable to everyone, in everything? He organised diversifications and set up units for each boy. Once the uncles had passed, remember how Bapu withdrew into his sanctuary in that temple he had built on the grounds and only let Arun see him?

'Why was Uma not with him, then? Because Ba had not invited her, so she never entered that place and the old man finally died without making peace? After that, Arun, with the consent of all the males had decided that the Big House be converted into a museum of family history downstairs, and be turned into a swanky Widows Home, upstairs. All the *bahus* were thrilled to have their *sasumas* out of their hair. Only Ba resisted and kept her apartment downstairs. Even Uma's Ma was sent there after her father's death, despite that 'dragon' downstairs!

'Now, how was Uma to meet her mother, if she couldn't step into the house without a formal invitation? Arun, my boy, I championed your cause with Uma all along. But now I'm tempted to regret it. She could have made herself comfortable in her own world. She had that talent. She came to you, but too soon, you went back to blowing up your 'elephant-in-the-room' obsessions to mammoth proportions. Were you actually looking for acknowledgement from a dumb elephant? She had allowed her husband to die instead! And she had the audacity to turn up here after Uma died?

'Everything you thought of, all that you did was aimed only as a jab at the nasty old lady. Did she also appear before your eyes when you were making love to Uma?' Abha said harshly, breathing heavily. The two men sat around her, breathing heavily. They were stunned at her outburst.

'Abha, how can you ...?'

'It is true, Achyut. Look at his record. He has always been fingering the old lady, never mind if the dart went past her to return to Uma. He would not invite her into the house even when he brought his father in. Not even after. Why? Because she had said she would not acknowledge the union. But she did turn up for the *Gruh Shanti*. Could never figure out how Bapu managed that! Would it not have been graceful just to take her in? She would have been shown to be a fool. But no, her words were more important than her actions, for the whole family, including his own father!

'Arun did you never think of how it must have hurt Uma, seeing you head to the Big House every single week for parties, pujas, festivals, births, deaths, birthdays, everything, fulfilling your duty as the eldest son! What about hers as the eldest *bahu*? You took her out in cars with darkened glass windows. You made some select appearances with her. What was that? Some inverted *purdah* decree by Ba?

'I admire Uma for rising to the challenge; she led her life, despite both, you and your bloody Ba. She held her head high and enjoyed putting her all into whatever she did.

'But I hated her for never letting you have it. That is what I am doing for her today. What do you deserve as a member of a family where all the males are mice waiting to be swatted by an elephant? Damn you!' She turned to leave, but Arun's voice stopped her.

'Wait Abha! Did Uma say all this to you?'

'Uma, talking against you? Don't you even know how crazy she was about you? No, she never uttered a word against you. But she did have a very expressive face and eyes, for those who looked with love. Why could you not read them, Arun, the shattered look on her face when you would trot off to the Big House and come and tell her about all your mischief there with great glee, not realising what an insult it was to her being! Yet she so graciously entertained all the relatives who chose to visit. She even kept silent when you took her mother to live there with Ba downstairs to rant at her, and that aunt who had a remote control-locked grill door installed to keep Ba out of her room.

'She kept herself busy while you took on everyone's jobs. Did you not realise that you were depriving her of your company, which was all she had, apart from Achyut and me—and even we've been away. What of your proud insistence of her receiving a formal invitation from Ba herself, never accepting that all your uncles, aunts and cousins had begged her to come home, even to the point when Bapu, himself, was calling out her name when he was facing death? Yes, Arun, I heard that and more than anger, I was ashamed. Ashamed that you could carry on a vendetta to such a level when you proclaimed you had no feelings whatsoever for that first wife, what was her name?'

Arun turned to Achyut with a tiny shake of his head.

'Hold it right there, Abha. When you don't hear from the horse's mouth, things can get distorted. I admit the earlier follies you listed, but the last—I never shared that with you, and it seems, neither did Uma. At that time, you both were abroad for International Arbitration courses. Let me tell you how Bapu died.'

His eyes looked bleak as he struggled with his tortured emotions. He had clasped his hands to control a slight tremor. Both Abha and Achyut were stunned at his reaction.

'When his youngest brother died young, Bapu was distraught. He wanted to get away. That's when he ordered his little temple built, with an adjoining room to which only he had the key. No one was allowed into the temple, except at his express invitation—not even Ba. In the house, he moved into a room across the house from hers, that looked out on his temple.

'It was a tiny, but superbly crafted temple with a spiraling low roof, marble *jhallis*, stark white marble with just a gleaming black Shivling in the centre. Nothing else. No *kanku*, no flowers, no *diyas*, no *agarbatis*, no bells. It was hidden behind hedges between the trees that shaded it and was disguised by a cunning, veiled gate on the side, away from the house. The gardener had precise instructions to prune the hedges and trees in every season to let in sunrays appropriately.

'Ba was strictly told not to enter—ever. He meditated, then rested in the adjoining room, sometimes all night. If anyone was troubled, he took them there and left. After dinner, he strolled barefoot on the lawn. As soon as Ba turned in, he slipped into his hideout.

'After a year, her son came to take *Kaki* to his home, but she refused and Ba ranted at her. That was when Bapu's patience finally broke. I was told he listed every single negative word and act of hers, an action that ended with not letting even his *bahu* enter his temple. He walked out, into his temple. Bansi *Kaka* found him sleeping on the floor with a raging fever. When he refused to get up, the old man called the uncles and me and made some *raab* to feed him. The doctor was called and while Bapu allowed him to give an injection, he refused to move from the floor.

'I rushed there and sat nursing him, his head on my lap, pleading with him. He asked about Uma, repeating her name every now and then. I would repeat what he would say and he'd close his eyes. Rudra came and we decided to take turns, so I came home to rest before going back for a night shift.' Arun stood up shakily, straightened his back and walked to the window, staring at the glass panes as if he was seeing the video of the incident in it.

'One day, I overslept, after the usual battle with Uma. When I woke, she was nowhere around. My worst fear was that Ba may have done something. I rushed but all was quiet in the house. In the temple, there was Uma, eyes closed as if in deep meditation. Her hands were on Bapu's head that lay in her lap. What was even more stunning was that after refusing a mattress or a blanket, Bapu was covered with her black shawl, sleeping with a peaceful look on his face.

'Rudra came out of the room where he was taking a nap, along with the doctor, while Uma alone kept vigil. But the fever had wreaked its damage. The doctor examined him once again and announced that it would not be long now. Rudra went to rouse the others in the house. Bapu breathed his last just before sunrise, with his head on Uma's lap, surrounded by his whole family, save Ba.

'By common consent, it was decided to bathe and dress him before taking him into the house for the rituals. No outsider, including Ba, would be told how and where he died. Uma herself had suggested that lest it become a source for universal gossip about her Vs. Ba. That night, after a long time, there was peace on her face when she slept without covering it with her arms. But I still shudder to think what would have been the outcome, had Ba taken it into her head to go out and visit him and seen him as I saw him—with his head in Uma's lap, his body shaking with fever.'

His eyes closed for a minute and Achyut moved to guide his trembling body back into his chair.

'What happened when Ba finally came?' Abha's voice was now gentler as her hand touched his shoulders.

Arun paused in sober recollection.

'Ah...how her face collapsed when she came out of her room and saw him covered with a sheet and flowers! The closed looks on all faces told her that no quarter would be given, just as she had never given us any. Her 'loving' bahu, Rudra's wife, Asha, didn't waste a minute in putting her hand out for the keys, saying that special food had to be made for the ceremonies.'

'And Ba handed over the keys, just like that?'

'I'm told she did and that's when the howling started. Thank god, we'd left, by then. Uma needed rest, especially after her long vigil, sitting cross-legged on that cold floor. As his heir, Rudra performed the rest of the last rites. We stayed out of sight to avoid a scene. Her satisfaction over that was loud and public.

'At the *besna*, Uma and I stood a little away from the family. I could hear the murmurs, but everyone bowed to us as they left. But it wasn't over yet.

'When the uncles, Rudra and his brother went for the immersion, they called the pundit who maintained our family records. Apparently, he had received strict, notarised written instructions from Bapu that his final rites were to be performed only by (after a heavy pause) his eldest son, Arun.

'Kaka rang me up to come at once. I left immediately with Uma. There was a particularly poor phone network there, so everyone here was awaiting their news and tempers were on a high. When Ba finally got through and heard that the immersion was held up, Rudra had to tell her the reason. I knew she would come here to rant, but she found a lock on the front door. I knew that I couldn't afford to leave Uma alone there.

'Despite that, Ba behaved sickly and knocked over some of the pots and destroyed the greenery in the veranda,' Arun said and finally paused. He was lost in thought, and sometimes, a tender smile would break out on his face.

'All this was sometime after you left for Europe for those special courses on International Arbitration. I wanted you both to get into a new branch of legal practice after the outburst Kiran had created in public. One needs to focus on a valuable practice in an era of growing international commerce,' he said. Once again, he paused.

Abha couldn't wait any longer to hear the rest. Impatiently, she shook him

'What happened after that?'

'What the Gods willed,' Arun said, almost smiling.

'When the tickets were booked, nobody noted that it was a hopping flight, Ahmedabad-Jaipur-Delhi. Jaipur is notorious for technical delays. By the time we landed at Delhi, Uma was exhausted, so we spent the night in a hotel there.'

That was the night when they should have been on their way home! Everything seemed to have let them down, phone lines, roads, traffic and even landing an efficient car.

'When the foothills could finally be seen, Uma was zapped by their beauty! She was totally fascinated by the natural loveliness around her, and she barely ate lunch, as she was too busy looking around. We reached in the early evening. By then, they'd almost given up on us and gone to see the Ganga aarti.

'We checked into a hotel. Then Uma and I sat on the opposite bank from where the sight was exquisite!

'Abha, imagine, the swift cool flow of the Ganga over your bare feet; across the water, hundreds of diyas floated in the current and a huge pyramid was being worked up by a pundit with the whole crowd singing and chanting. It is raucous and loud, up close, but across the banks, the Ganga waters had mellowed the sound, making it very pleasing to the ears.

'We held hands to ward off the chill, absorbing the beauty of the little glow caused by the reflecting dots of light in the water, echoed by those in the black sky above.

After a while, we could see lights scattered high up in hill homes, too. It was heady! The sounds of rushing water and that cold breeze!'

Arun took a deep breath and waited a long time before he resumed his narrative.

'Next morning, the ceremonial duty was duly completed. We prayed for Bapu's soul to find peace in the next life; I almost asked whether he would meet my mother there.

'Uma went through with it all, her glances alternating between me, the flowing river, and the majestic mountains. She couldn't resist that.'

A smile flashed on his face, reminding them of the old Arun.

'While we were waiting for lunch at the Ashram, I found that she had vanished. A young ashramite pointed towards the river flowing below the ashram. Wordlessly, I joined her there and seated myself next to her. Peace descended on us in the semi-darkness. Soon, the bright sunlight faded and it was dark.

'There were steps running along the width of the building going down into the water, and one can sit on a dry step with feet immersed in the cool water, meditating. The flow of the water in the shadows, the building blocking out the sights of the bazaar just opposite and the noise of the vendors. It was an amazing spot.

'After a while, the uncles also joined us, enchanted by

the same magic,' said Arun as he finally fell silent reliving his memories. His two friends sat by his side, waiting for him to come back to the present.

'The long and short of it was that Uma decided she would stay at least for a week, at a hotel or ashram, to breathe in the river and the mountains. All of us agreed, except Rudra; we told him to go to take up his MD duties. I could handle International from wherever I was. We all needed this break.'

'We moved to a hotel as the elderly uncles needed their comfort. That led to a proposal for a family home there, which morphed into a hotel with one suite reserved for family permanently. Kaka went a step further, adding, 'If it works out, make it into a franchise.'

After lunch, Uma's adventures came up again.

'The trip was truly memorable. We roamed the bazaars, ghats, mountains, snowy tops, green forests and streams. I don't remember when Uma had ever smiled so much. 'We were drifting over hills and dale, as it were; at night, she would cuddle against me with the sweetest smile,' he said, closing his eyes as he dreamily recalled that exquisite time.

'That week was a gift of tranquility that held us up through the Will reading, that retained me as the Head of the family after him with overall veto power. It also decreed handing deeds to those whose houses had been built on the estate, with the proviso of no sale for property development to anyone outside the family.

'Rudra was now stuck in the house with a powerless Ba, who now turned viciously against two victims, Rudra and Uma. Finally, I met her to reassure her that Rudra was doing Bapu proud as MD. Guess what she said to me during that meeting?' continued Arun. After a long pause, he resumed talking.

'You know what she said to me? "Now that Jinal is gone, why don't you marry that one and make her a proper wife?"'

'She said what?' shouted Abha, as both she and Achyut reacted visibly.

'You heard me. God help me, I almost raised my hand to slap her hard. But Uma's guiding spirit held my hand back. When I finally told Uma about this, she wasn't happy either.'

'What's the use now? Bapu is not there. Let us remain happy as we are, rather than letting her crow.'

Quietly, another canker matured. Uma suddenly found herself bereft of energy. Possibly it was menopause approaching. She complained of pains, shedding responsibilities and obviously, depression began to set in. They'd return happily from a cheery trip, all perked up, only to slide back into depression once at home. All the tests in the world could not throw up any specific diagnosis, until finally they were directed to head to Chandigarh to check out what seemed a spot in her uterus.

'With all her extensive reading, at some stage, Uma turned to alternative treatment. We heard of a miracle cure....'

'No, Arun, not you! Uma possibly, but how could you?'

'Listen. I was desperate; Uma was fading away in front of me. Could I afford to lose her? Here was a qualified psychotherapy counsellor with knowledge of various alternate sciences dealing with emotional and physical ailments, that are often not diagnosable in laboratories. We read that the whole of one's psyche has a role to play along with subconscious mental triggers, possibly connected to a previous life.

'With no definitive medical diagnosis in hand yet, we thought it would not harm us to give it a shot. When we finally reached our destination, an ordinary cottage with a potted garden in an old world society and a lady with a beatific smile, Maya, leaning at the gate, greeted us cheerily, saying, 'I've had the feeling that somebody would come by today. Good to see you.'

'We were dazed—she was that intuitive. Firmly but gently, she listened to each of us, individually first, then together in a simple sanctuary; then she offered us her diagnosis. She said that some deep-rooted issues needed resolutions. She assured us that there would be no lectures, no meds, only counselling "to see what we are up against".

'I needed time to think about it, but you know Uma, her eyes and her plaintive smile? When she emerged after a while, she seemed more at peace with herself. That night she slept well.'

Maya insisted that I needed sessions first, to open myself up; then only could I give Uma the support she would need. A couple of sessions endorsed what Abha intuitively knew: the Ba obsession was the big holdup.

Maya wisely let him draw the same conclusion for himself. Then, after some opening sessions, Maya prescribed a carefully selected flower remedy that in a short while, showed a notable change in Uma's outlook and stamina levels. Reluctant to reveal their 'alternative therapy experiences' to sceptic medicos, they let them claim the credit. Maya had pre-warned them.

'This was after you'd started those International Arbitration courses in Europe, to prepare for fresh opportunities in the new international commerce era.'

Arun told his two old friends that he moved his office into the newly constructed office building within the home complex, to be closer to Uma during the days as well.

'We took another break, this time in Coorg. There were hills for miles around, and days of rain and mists, peaks dotted by clouds. There was the dozing sun, wind and the rich aromas of coffee and honey and curry leaves in the food. Uma loved it all. But we got soaked, not once but twice.

The first time, we took it lightly and came back to change in front of a cosy fire and some hot brandy to drive the chill away. Uma woke up the next day, pulled on her warm dressing gown and sat on the veranda, watching a pair of squirrels scrambling on the boundary wall, merry patrolling sentries, while hidden birds chirped overhead in the tallest branches of the trees.

'What d'you think, are those gossip updates or warnings of danger?' she asked. Pigeons cooed, taking off and returning like lost souls. 'Are they the same ones who just went, or different?' I was amazed at her keen observations on nature.

Rain drenched us on the hills the second time, and her fever shot up. I panicked and brought her right back. This time, it took her longer to pull out of it.

'If she was improving, what happened? How did Uma die?' Abha burst out.

Tears filled Arun's eyes. 'Remembering her nature fascination, I got a little puppy to surprise her with. She was coming down the stairs with her usual grace when she spotted me, pup in my arms.

Excitedly she scampered down and slipped; I wasn't fast enough to catch her or break her fall and her head knocked against the last step.'

The friends closed in, arms woven giving succour to each other, mourning the lost partner.

Kaushalya's Story

Kaushalya appeared at the gates of the massive bungalow. Her piercing glance and voice finally led her into the presence of Motiba Sahib, who was heading for her nap. Adjusting her *pallu*, she touched Motiba's toes in a show of respect, but the latter's face was a map of disdain.

'Who are you? Why are you here?'

'Motiba Sahib, I am Kaushalya. Post-Partition, we came here to work hard to rebuild our lives, not to loot or be looted. As a family elder, I have come to you for justice.'

'Go to a judge for justice. I am not a judge.'

The reply was soft but unsympathetic.

'Your family will rue the day I go to a judge for this justice.' Her arm cradled her belly. The old lady was taken aback, her face showing disdain.

'Should I believe any girl who wanders in?' she replied, sternly. 'Do you know what can become of you?'

'Motiba, I reached you here. So, we can do a lot to each other. But would that solve the problem? All I asked your nephew was for money for the abortion. Did he tell you that?'

Looking keenly into the older woman's eyes, she read her ignorance. 'Your Manek. What will happen to the child of an unmarried mother, a refugee? I refuse to accept that fate for me or my child.'

Motiba's chutzpah was certainly shocked. She spat out, 'Anyone will come here and bark about my boys and I should believe?'

'Not anyone, this is me, Kaushalya,' she tugged at the black thread at her neck pulling out a ring tucked out of sight. 'Recognise this? I have other things too!'

'Why didn't you sell them?'

'Sell your family into bazaar gossip?' Motiba recognised the checkmate move.

Silence reigned for some minutes. Finally, she spoke, 'Go now. Let me speak to him first.' She motioned to her old maid to escort Kaushalya out, who noticed the exchange between Motiba and the maid.

'Remember, if you take too long, abortion will not be an option.' Outside the door, she stopped deliberately to adjust her pallu and looked around. At the edge of the stairs, she motioned the other to step down first, smiling.

'You are older,' she told Motiba, effectively nixing any intention the older woman might have had of pushing her down those stairs forcibly.

'None of your tricks on Bahenji,' growled two strapping young men who appeared out of nowhere; a small crowd stood watch outside the gate.

Post-Partition, large convoys of Sindhi refugees had poured in from across the border and later settled far beyond the mill owners' massive bungalows and the sprawling cantonment. Intrepid Sindhis poured into town, looking for work; the city men-about-town preyed on their young women. Kaushalya, an English graduate back in those days, sought work, too, but ended up knocked up at the hands of one of the Family.

Not one to take things lying down, she collared the fellow, but he escaped. The next day, Kaushalya appeared at the gates of the massive bungalow. Her piercing glance and voice won her entry.

That evening, a stern-faced Uncle Govindram had a visitor, a family emissary who spoke in whispers in a tin-roofed room. She listened to the exchange. They wanted more proof than just that one ring. In response to his unspoken query, Kaushalya held out a closed fist.

The uncle crisply reminded the emissary: 'You know, after this, she will not get any proposals. Her whole life has been jeopardised. Do you understand that? You have two days to decide; then we will file the case with all the reports and then the abortion will happen. If you want the child,'—this last was accompanied by an unyielding look, '...you people will have to look after the mother for a whole year, along with her protectors. We want our daughter alive.'

Before he left the camp, the emissary 'encountered' two other gentlemen who were advising the negotiators, 'We're experienced traders. Our people operate globally where your mills could export. Why wreck business for one small thing? Think big!'

Reeling in confusion, he returned to brief the family elders, recounting both conversations, one with the uncle and the other with the two traders. The men stroked their chins, thoughtfully.

'Makes sense. Local markets will take time to revive after these communal troubles. Exports are an excellent option, more so in the long run.'

Kaushalya vanished for a week, then came back, a little pale, with an appointment letter and a fixed deposit certificate in her bag. Her brothers refused the appointment letters in favour of setting up a shop. Soon, the market was booming with new traders setting up shop. Kaushalya reigned for decades as the mills' custodian of the files, safely out of sight.

After a while, like many others, she too moved into one of the many mill chawls in the city. It was closer to work, and there was far less expense on transport. To supplement her income, she gave English tuitions, helping Gujarati children and others from the community to improve their pronunciations and understanding.

At the mill, where she lived in the basement with her files, she remained out of sight and after a while, was out of memory, except for a handful of people.

Among her students, one was particularly close to her heart; this was a deprived little girl with a yearning for learning. One day, she found her sitting outside her window, quietly mouthing the spelling and enunciating the words that she had taught her and other students.

'What are you doing here?'

Startled, the little one rebounded quickly, 'Listening,' she replied.

'Why?' Kaushalya asked her, even as she saw tears appear in the little girl's eyes.

'Sorry. My family cannot afford the fees for me.'

But Kaushalya had already seen the spark in the little one's eyes. She continued to let her listen in, till she worked out a barter system with her mother. Meals would replace the tuition fees, and that would ease Kaushalya's burden of cooking.

Uma, her little protégé did her proud with her easy command over the language; she later pushed her to learn stenography so that eventually, it was easier to organise a job for her at the same mill where her father and grandfather had worked.

Kaushalya always stayed under the radar in the basement.

THERE WAS a buzz: a daughter of the family was getting married and festivals were around the corner. Would that mean a bigger bonus for the workers this year?

In the midst of it all, news broke out of Manek's death in a drunken brawl. Whatever he had so far done to earn the title of the Family's Black Sheep, he was still a part of the family. A private cremation was followed by a traditional *Besna* (condolence meeting).

It was reflection time for Kaushalya, who found herself shriveled up in shock, thinking of the only man who had ever courted her, touched her and pampered her; and had then mercilessly thrown her to the wolves so devastatingly that she was almost forced to withdraw herself from the world. Fury and longing tore at her all night through.

Morning, however, brought clarity. If she stayed away, she would be totally forgotten. Who knows, her job and that fixed deposit (that now seemed so meagre after decades) may also somehow be snatched away to make room for a fresher. After all, the younger generation probably knew nothing about this particularly unhappy escapade of their uncle.

Perhaps she had to go, not to condole or feel sorry for

his terrible death, but to remind the Family that they still owed her. Let the younger folk now wonder and ask about her presence at a family function.

Glancing across the landing at Uma's, she recalled her people had been with the mill for a long time, but it did not look like anyone was heading for the *Besna*. Was Manek not an important part of the mill?

Steeling herself for the upcoming ordeal, she added dark glasses to her face to offset her sober white sari and headed out.

The Besna was not well-attended. Many of the Family were conspicuous by their absence.

A solitary stern-faced figure sat alone, dark glasses sheltering her eyes, behind two rows of empty chairs.

Vishal, who ran the show hands-on, was taken aback at seeing Kaushalya at the Besna that so many family members, too, had given a miss. She was the only one who had not come to the table to pick up the flower petals to shower over the portrait; she had just sat there, bowed her head from afar, and walked out. What was she thinking? Was she cursing or mourning a loss?

His lawyer friend, Subodh jogged his memory.

'Miss File Custodian, isn't she?'

'You know her? Why is she here? She didn't come for the festivals or the wedding.'

'*Yaar* Vishal, did Europe make you dense or was it America? She is Kaushalya, isn't she?' Shifting to a quiet corner, the story finally tumbled out. It was Vishal's Dad who had organised the resolution.

The next day, Vishal had headed downstairs to the basement, rather than up to his office.

'Good morning, Miss Kaushalya. How are you?' he said, observing her still looking pale and strained. 'I'm truly sorry. I can only imagine what negative emotions must have been dredged up yesterday. Can we put it behind us now, please?'

'Who has sent you?' she asked; her voice sounded suspicious.

'No one. I represent myself only. As colleagues, can we maintain a separate equation?' his voice said gently. 'I came to ask you for an update on the progress of your protégé, Miss Dalal. How is she doing?'

'You seem inordinately interested in her progress, Mr Vishal. Why?'

'Naturally. She is an asset to my office. It would be more valuable if she is able to handle important guests, including those coming from abroad. Also, it would entail a big hike in her take-home pay, if she did that. That would be useful for her family too, I understand?' he said, while addressing her with a raised eyebrow.

'Is that all?' Her eyes narrowed. 'Uma is well-trained now to carry off anything expected of her. I can guarantee that. As regards the other matter, since her saris are now pretty well-worn, maybe a generous pay hike will enable her to undertake a shopping spree soon to rectify that as well.'

Resisting the temptation to ask why she had abstained from all the celebrations, Vishal nodded his thanks and headed up.

That was the day he called in Priscilla, his staff-in-charge. He asked her directly, 'How did Uma get this job?'

'She's the third generation in our office, sir. Please check the file.'

Looking around embarrassed, she added, 'Just call for all the ladies' files.'

Priscilla was well-known to Kaushalya and later, she recounted her conversation with Vishal. The request drew Kaushalya's curiosity, who remarked, 'My, my, what's happening upstairs?'

'Perhaps someone wants to do something for us, ladies,' Priscilla replied pertly.

Kaushalya stood up to peer out of the window, turning her head from side to side.

'What are you looking for?'

'Cinderella's Godmother's coach,' came the sardonic reply, before both burst out laughing at the thought.

Fortune Hunters

He opened the covering note that had come with the papers he had received.

It read:

Subodh,
Since you've been hearing the story from both, Baap 'n' Beti, you might want to read the last entries, Anil had written before he died.
Shobha Grover'

Subodh thought at once about a dissolute drinker who haunted the bar.

He opened the file and flipped over to the covering page:

Monday

This evening, I ran into Subodh, sloshing down a bottle at the club.

'Hit the gym, man,' he rallied, 'not the bottle.'

'I am drowning my sorrows. Fortune hunters everywhere are after my girl.'

'What fortune?"

'She's working towards it; she runs my business now.'

'As you once did?' he asked

'I didn't have the energy to make it. She will, if she stays out of their clutches.'

'Whose?'

'Fortune hunters.'

Subodh walked off.

Tuesday

Subodh asked, 'Still drowning in sorrow?'

'My dad gave me a bang-up education, an office and left me on my own with Rupees twenty-five lakhs. Not an amount to sneeze at, back then.'

'And?'

'Ran through it.'

'All of it?'

'Bad business debts. So, he ensured my marriage to Miss Moneybags.'

'Ah, the fortune hunter....'

'She wasn't.'

'You were. Right?' Subodh said, as he walked away.

Wednesday

'They're circling around my girl; they are leeches eyeing our business and money.'

'How do you know?'

'My dad left his all to Mom. Pa-in-law to my girl.'

'Then it's hers, not yours.'

'Listen Man…. Smart fellows show her doggie eyes, fuck her and….'

'Then?'

'Don't marry her. One walked out afterwards. But all eye the….'

'But, where's the fortune, man? Didn't it go in bad debts?'

'Aw, life carries on. A business has to be run, and property bought and sold. Who pays for this club and drinks?'

I walked off.

Thursday

'Cheers!'

'Still drinking? What happened to the business after property was bought and sold?' asked Subodh.

'What has business to do with drinks?'

'With fortune hunters then?'

'Those guys just will not let go of my poor baby, sucking her dry, financially.'

'What about, emotionally?'

'That too. But my concern is that she should not let go of the business.'

'Listen to this, Anil. My daughter had two criteria: looks and money. She found them in the Thakur of a small estate and married him pronto. Guess what she found back home?'

'What?"

'The title and fortune were courtesy of his elder brother, who married his heart ala Edward VIII. His grandfather disowned him. But, for his people, he remains *Bade Thakur*, his wife is *Didi Thakurain*. The Thakurain title tastes bitter now for the poor girl.'

Subodh walked off.

Friday

Today, it was the daughter who was drinking.

'So you were the *bakra* this time. Has Dad convinced you of the Siege of the Fortune Hunters, of which he was the original hero?'

'So?'

'Did he tell you that I lost one boyfriend who called me a Pa-Xerox and another a Mom Clone? My husband walked out when he found I was too busy with Dad's business to have a baby.'

'Is it that bad?'

'Moneywise, not bad. But it's a time guzzler. I had no

time for him, so where was the time to look after a kid?'

'So now?'

'I'm looking for a guy who'll run or subsidise Dad's business so I can do other things.'

The daughter walked off.

Ruefully, Subodh slipped the papers back into his pocket.

Kashmir Trilogy

A YELLOW ROSE

She stood at a terrace window watching an interaction between the veggies and flower boat*wallas* with some hesitant clients in the early morning. These were townsfolk looking for cheap deals as resources were limited and no one knew where the next bit of income would come from.

Ironically, even those who had resources, bought little. Who knew, a show of it might mean you would soon be hounded by the authorities! That meant that flower sellers got short shrift. They had no time for luxurious blooms.

An old man with an awkward gait that spelt pain, inched closer, picking up two radishes, and a small fistful of greens.

No one questioned his limited choice.

They knew the circumstances. An old couple riddled with illness, with perhaps the wife on her deathbed.

The old man paused to look, taking in the gentle movement in the lake waters that allowed the sun's rays to create a variety of shades of blue-green. Patterns of the serene blue sky lit up the waters of the Dal Lake, at places backed by a flowing plateau of hills; majestic, white-topped mountains were seen in the distance. At the centre of the Lake bloomed green plantations with veggies and flowers. Alongside was a ghost town of empty houseboats.

Nostalgia and pain swept across the old face as he thought, 'How she would have loved this *nazara*! We used to come here together every day as long as she could.'

His eyes swept across the small crowd of boatsellers, zeroing in on the ones with rainbows of fresh blooms. For a moment, his eyes lit up, and then a question flitted onto his face.

'Can we afford it?'

Then he made up his mind and beckoned to one, who thrilled to have his first customer of the day, held up an array of different bouquets. The old man shook his head.

'Don't you have any yellow flowers?' he asked hesitantly. The young man was swift in picking out a bunch of them, showing off their freshness, with the morning dew still glistening on some petals. Doubt rose again on the old man's face.

'*Beta*, I only want one flower—a yellow one only.' He seemed to hesitate over what seemed his poor choice. The seller's face fell.

'Kaka, take the bunch, I'll give you a good discount...' But the old man's voice firmed.

'Only one good yellow bloom.'

Then the voice pleaded, 'Please, she is ill and she only likes yellow ones. I have to go back fast so she can see the dewdrops before she goes.'

Several others turned to watch him, curiously. The seller graciously selected the freshest of his blooms, rolled it in cellophane paper and held it out to his customer, who quickly held out a folded note.

There were tears in the eyes of the forlorn flower seller.

'No Kaka, this flower is a gift from me. I shall pray for her, too; and before she goes, ask her to pray that my little ones survive this winter.'

Despite the brutalisation, as daily tragedies roamed afield, Srinagar had not lost all of its serenity and soul.

The old man trotted home as fast as he could go, the yellow flower shielded by a paper offered by one of the other sellers, to protect the dewdrops from the sun. He called out to her from the doorstep:

'See what I got for you,' he said, while handing over the yellow flower to his forlorn wife.

She gave him a tender little smile with an effort, but could not lift her hand, so he placed it where she could smell its fragrance.

Then he went to wash his feet and swiftly put away his meagre purchases.

When he came back, her eyes were glazed, gazing at the flower, a dew drop on her still lips.

Land of Beauty
Of smiling Gardens
Land of Sorrow
And bygone Ruins.

Ancient and mystical
Mir'd in mists of Time
A history so bountiful
A present sadly mauled
By insecure offspring
Bent on erasing Past.

Did no hoary seer
Foresee this tragedy?
And brew its antidote?
That thy beauty is
As accursed as that
Of a Beautiful Woman.

THE SECOND SHOT
'Aah, at last,' the gentleman got out, moved into the sun and stretched expansively. The drive from the airport

had been a long and exhausting one.

A blooming resort nestled in the gentle hills, topped with dense verdant trees. Elegant settings and delicious food amidst the floral kingdom were on offer to the guests. But he was among those who sought the refuge of solitude and serenity in the minuscule sit-outs, soaking in an early winter sun amidst fresh fragrances and the sight of large, multihued marigolds and asters, through the open windows that surrounded his sit-out.

The marigolds were absolutely different from the saffron and yellow ones in the plains. Here they bloomed, palm-sized, in an amazing variety of colours and hues to offer rainbow marigold beds awash with morning and evening dews, their pungent smell protecting the surrounding delicate flowers from predatory insects.

His keen eyes took in the serenity of the scene, the floral range, the greens waving in the gentle breeze, a cloudless sky overhead embroidered with feathery, white plume strands turning bulbous as they approached the horizon hidden behind wooded hills.

He stared for so long, standing absolutely still that even a passer-by stopped to ask:

'Saab, sab theek to hai?' Shaken out of his reveries over the natural magnificence, he could not do more than merely nod his head fervently.

It was the hills that stood out most in the mind's eye, rising gracefully in tiers, eternal custodians of the whole, enclosing the houses as if offering a sanctuary to nestle in. Wasn't that so?

His sharp ears picked up a soft rustle. He rose to lean against the railing, breathing deeply as if taking in the sight. But his keen eyes had already felt, rather than seen the bushes move ever so slightly; then, in the distance, a small hidden gate creaked softly.

His eyes followed the elusive movements heading for the dense tree cover high on the hills.

Averting his eyes, he looked up at the wooded hills, again; this time not seeing their beauty, but assessing the shadows cast by the treetops and what they might be hiding. Those woods seemed particularly dense; from the distance, nothing was visible.

'Is that a sanctuary for them? Who? For the locals? From across the border, or further up?' his thoughts wandered. 'What prompts them to rape these hills, so like theirs in the northern homeland,' he wondered. Were these paid mercenaries? Were the locals hesitant to wreck their own homeland, so they preferred the services of mercenaries?

Those northern lands too suffered, as they had for centuries, at the hands of alien rapists fighting over it tooth and nail. Now they want to gift the same to another beautiful land?

He straightened his shoulders and maintained a vigil. His mind meanwhile cast around for whom he could safely contact, someone trustworthy in the maze of relationships, politics, alignments, and economics that had riddled a war-torn society for decades.

A pair of vigilant eyes zeroed in on him from an attic window high above, across the courtyard.

In the far distance, on a hilltop that he had concentrated on, he thought he saw a movement. Then came the doubt: was it a human movement or that of the tree's cape of leaves? Swiftly as the breeze rose, sure enough, the capes of the trees egged each other on, swaying in graceful unison to the pull of the wind that swirled all the way in, to finally ruffle the watcher's hair too. A rueful smile creased his lips.

'What a fool I'm being! This is Paradise on Earth and I've wasted the day looking for shit instead of breathing in the beauty.'

Another day dawned and then yet another day, each with its own cloud formations, hilltop shadows and floral displays that tugged at his heart when he walked to the dining room for meals. He was determined not to become a reclusive hermit and order only room service.

It felt good to dress up for dinner, even though only two or three tables were occupied. It felt good to smile expansively at fellow guests and pinch the cheeks of little ones who, once in a while, trotted over with a smile.

The mild sunshine encouraged him to face the outdoors to once again face those magnetic hills, his face and shoulders shielded by a large sunshade. His mind went back for a minute to his enforced rest after his surgery to remove a bullet. 'Was it really stray?'

It had been a rare golf morning with his superior. As he angled his shot, his eye was distracted by a golf cart moving leisurely down the driveway, driven by a young man with a silver-haired companion. He pondered over the strange pair, wondering what they were doing on this elegant golf course. The old lady looked around her with sheer delight on her face, her short hair unabashedly buoyed by the breeze in all directions and a broad, amused smile creasing her face whenever she turned to share her joy at the surroundings with the young man by her side. Then they turned into a path into a denser, wooded area.

Later, he again caught a glimpse of them and almost shouted out at their foolhardiness: the path cut through steep slopes on both sides, neither side negotiable for the golf cart. And the sprinkler was on full blast.

The cart stopped a few metres away. Bemused, he watched as they conferred for some minutes; he drew swiftly closer, but remained in the shadow of the trees, so they knew not that someone was listening. Or watching.

'Mom,' the young man said, 'We'll have to turn away for a long detour or wait anywhere from fifteen to thirty minutes before the sprinkler changes direction. Want to wait it out or turn?'

The old woman, now identified as Mom shook her head. '*Beta*, my back is tired now. I want to sit and relax somewhere, but the grass here must be wet.' A little conference later, he saw the golf cart crashing through the sprinkler to emerge with two thoroughly wet souls laughing their heads off.

'Mom, I never knew you to be so adventurous...' the voice rang out loud as they strove to swipe down as much water as possible, still laughing at the memory of that heady rush. Those couple of seconds must have soaked them through, he thought as they sped away.

It was at that moment that he felt a jolt between his shoulders. Instinctively, he bent to avoid the next and saw a gush of blood on the ground. The golf cart had already vanished around the next bend. Within seconds, his golf partner and their men reached him.

'Was it them? The old lady?'

One afternoon, he hit the jackpot! There was that now familiar and the gentlest of rustles followed by a noiseless opening and shutting of the hidden gate. A shadow moved away, with a gentleman in hot pursuit, swinging his arm to loosen it after the recent surgery. He reminded himself once again that he was to try no unnecessary stunts! His pace was swift as the target almost floated—a veiled ghost moving through thick tree cover, knowing exactly where to place his feet for a firm grip, without faltering. He inched closer and closer; finally, putting his hand out to grasp the shroud roughly by the neck.

'*Ya* Allah!' the words escaped, perhaps, involuntarily from the figure.

He got a sudden, mental jolt. Was this a female?

While he absorbed the shock, she shook off the shroud and the skull cap, but the grip on her collar was more determined.

Swiftly, black-covered figures appeared, their faces, unseen. The Other watched from afar. A net crashed onto the Watcher from overhead; the Cloaks led the woman away swiftly, not only for safety but also because they had seen what the Watcher had missed: a swirling mist that soon swamped the sight of the fleeing figures and left him in a cloud.

He stood perfectly still, taking his bearings; when he realised the net was gone—in that mist? He tried to recall the path that had brought him here. He trotted warily, hoping it was the correct direction, till the lights of the resort twinkled, beckoning him back to his room. The Other followed, tailing him unseen.

JHAROKHA

'Aapa, dekho. They're there again.'

'Kitne?' (How many?)

'Two.'

I scurried to catch the oft-repeated sight we'd observed off and on for some days now from my little wooden *jharokha* that protruded into a crowded bazaar, high above across the road and up the little hill.

It wasn't a very large window; it was rectangular, taller than it was wider, so only two could look out of it, unless an occasional child peered over the bottom, presumably perched between the elders. The jharokha seemed quite jail-like, close-set and sturdily designed, carved out of thick, crisscrossing wood, denying entry or exit of anything, except air. Veiled faces, with only the eyes being visible flitted back and forth all day. Were they keeping a vigil, I wondered.

It was a world of veils; the irony of the situation was that in the highly conservative setting, even the males sought veils, albeit of a different kind.

The women covered their heads and drew it across the lower half of their face too, leaving only the eyes visible.

And the men? They made a fashion statement with their woollen monkey caps, rolled up around their ears—that they could pull down in a blink, to cover the whole face, even the lips. They would tuck in their caps into the collar of their kurta. No skin was visible, and all one could see were only eyes and nostrils. Kurtas, salwars, gloves, socks and the ubiquitous sports shoes made something of a uniform to compete with the starch and spit of the soldiers on duty, perhaps.

My jharoka, which is usually described as a window fronted by carved wooden grill either single or to form a little jutting alcove, must once have been quite attractive. But, bereft of regular maintenance and oiling in these hard times, its wood had deteriorated, the carvings worn, and its colours bleached to shades of grey and black. Ditto that of the other windows that also overlooked the bazaar; even the walls surrounding it seemed to be crying for a coat of paint.

Suddenly, a hubbub broke out below. The melee of vendors and hawkers swiftly melted away as a jeep sped through, followed by soldiers. Their sight triggered off the usual sounds. Could it be called a barrage? Hardly so, perhaps, it was a smattering? From apparently nowhere, some stones dropped out of the sky at random, the throwers not knowing whether they would hit any target. Was it just for effect?

As the soldiers primed, what was till then, sporadic, became a minor fusillade: some figures could be seen, their faces covered by monkey caps to defy identification; they were now flinging the stones with more precision, but these were still falling woefully short as they kept a wary eye on the advancing soldiers, and judged their escape through the narrow lanes. This ragtag army was born and bred there, and figured their chances were definitely better those alien soldiers with their clumsy heavy boots and guns. They knew the area and could jump and leap off and drop out of sight at will.

Watching from my eyrie, it seemed almost a game; waves of loose-limbed human monkeys would vanish into quickly open-and-shut doors, move up to hop terraces to another place altogether that had not seen any stone pelting. A wet cloth wiped off all signs of battle, a swift change of clothes and transformation into an errand boy or student from a college or madrassa, while the stones were quickly 'confiscated'. Then others took the field.

'Does that help? Confiscating the stones? Is there any shortage of stones in the hilly countryside that is denuded of tree cover, orchards and fields?'

The little play would be staged again and again; sometimes just without a plan. There was hot blood on one side that was itching to show off foolhardiness, but it meant that they could hurt someone else caught in the crossfire. At other times, it was done purposely to draw attention away from something happening elsewhere. That's how guerrilla warfare is conducted, isn't it? Shivaji was an expert in it!

The word out later was that some militants had left, while others made it in. Monkey caps and uniform coloured salwar-kurtas make for an excellent disguise. Some had been accommodated further afield, where no one would dream of ever looking for them.

I too scurried to safety, right out of the old city into its 'modern' twin, with its wide boulevards, colourful gardens, high-walled security-fenced fortresses, ambitious residences with flowing fountains and grand staircases testifying that like the rest of the world, everywhere else, there were those who didn't feel the pinch. Cocktails and kebabs flowed in gracious settings that had people performing *shayari* on mellow evenings. It was there that my mind flew to a Stone Pelting *ka Purana Khiladi* (an old hand at stone pelting), in my hometown of Ahmedabad. And a new line of thought arose:

Dear Stone Pelters of Kashmir
Do you know your stones?
Their shape, their size,
Their feel or their weight?
The ones that only nick
Those that hurt or push back?
Can you identify them as we do?
Have you ever gone back?
To bring them home for next time?

When the Masis (aunts) go to collect
Just before sundown
They identify their own
And those of others too.
'Lila, this is scratched. Yours, no?
If you see Bela tell her the crosswala
Is near the blue light, with her grey one
I'm still looking for my dented one
You know, the small smooth one....'

We've had ours for generations!
Grew up with little piles, living
Permanently on our terraces

In the Pols.
You?

From
The Stone Pelters of Ahmedabad

The charms of the blooming gardens could not hold me for long; I headed back to my jharokha lookout. Just in time...the next thing we knew, we were prisoners in our own town, not even able to connect with family.

Who came?

Food On The Table

The post-coital glow blossomed radiantly on her mature face. He gazed at it in wonder.

How could such a scrawny body, those thin limbs with long feet hide such lusty abandon?

He had glimpsed her twice, striding purposefully into HR to pose queries at various desks, the last meaningful enough to land in his internal mail.

The name was unknown...Shubra Nayyar, and her LinkedIn profile was meagre.

He never knew what caught his attention, maybe it was just her outrageous logic. Purposely he had walked through, ears perked to hear her out as she harangued someone or the other in the HR department. Her unshapely cotton saris and silvered dark hair got a derisive glance from him.

'Union activist type,' he thought dismissively when he saw her closely.

She was busy demanding of someone, 'You must...you must listen to me.'

He found out later that her sister had been dismissed after repeated warnings from the HR. But her job had put food on their table.

Soon, he was at the receiving end of her complaints. He listened with one ear, his eyes sizing her up lazily. At the first stirrings in his loins, he wondered, 'Would she be good?'

He couldn't remember how he managed it, yet here they were in bed together after an amazingly high soar, sky high...with Madam Cotton Sari!

She stirred. Looking up, her eyes widened at him; then a slow smile spread across her face, tentatively, widening at his quick response.

'Shuhra, you really pack a punch, sweetheart,' he smiled, unctuously.

Her eyes lowered, as she bit her lower lip. He almost gasped.

As she sat up, her hair cascaded down. Thin, stick-like arms sped up to wind it into a bun that rose high on her head, making her almost goddesslike.

'Who, no, what are you? Fairy, nymph, or Aphrodite?' He asked bemused, as she pulled a corner of her sari to slither it over her breasts, before turning to give him a smile.

'Does it really matter? You got what you wanted. Now

give my sister her job back.'

'I thought it was given and taken right here. Once more?' he beguiled.

She looked at him from top to toe pointedly as she stood up, proudly naked. 'You overestimate yourself, Sir,' she said with some emphasis. 'Maybe some other time?' The indifference and cocked eyebrow sent his blood to his face. Icy shards shot from his eyes.

'How much?'

She looked up at him while pleating her sari.

'Re-appointment letter. Now. And no shim sham later, mind you.'

'And if I've taped you?'

'I have you,' she said, giving him a tight smile. Then, sitting on his couch, crossing her legs, she swung her slippered foot.

Panic-stricken, he looked around quickly, narrowing at her purse nearby. He lunged.

'Bingo,' she said, clapping her hands, 'but the master's somewhere else. So, letter please. Pronto,' she said, glancing at her watch.

'What's the hurry, sweetie? Stick around a bit,' he said while picking up his mobile.

'Look, this is business. Letter now. I have another client to service and you've overshot your timeline.' As his mouth sagged, he thanked his lucky stars that his back was towards her.

Walking out after tucking the letter neatly into her bag, her mouth drooped.

'He was not an evil person. But business is business. This'll put food on my table too.'

She drew herself up, head up, consoling herself with this argument.

Does Age Matter?

They were perfectly matched, yet different. There was a flurry of speculation among both their close pals and the wider circle. Would it happen? Or...?

They had been together at a Seniors' Group Tour in the foothills. Spring was out in full form and colour, cool, yet warm. On the way back, RS placed his hand on Jaya's on the divider between their bus seats, only to have her snatch hers firmly away. A low voice spoke gently:

'It was only to feel that tender hand once, Jaya.'

'I... just don't like being touched.' Looking away, her mind zoomed into the past, holding back bitter tears, shying away from relationships. At some point, it floated through, 'When he's gone, why cling to his words?'

Morning saw a rejuvenated Jaya heading for Manorama's.

'Mano, I need help. I'm tired of being half woman.'

'Jaya, what do you mean by half-woman?'

It was confession time as Jaya began to recall her disastrous marriage, from being a bride to being eternally pregnant, often used as a pumping machine. Frequent abortions had left her a physical and mental wreck until the final insult, when he said, 'I can't swim in you anymore.'

When the sobbing would not stop, she found herself being slapped tightly.

'You have shed enough tears for a lifetime. It could have been taken care of ages ago, *buddu*. Come on now, Late *Latif*.'

'Where?'

'You'll find out, you soon-to-be-whole-woman. Come!'

Reassurance came from the doctor who promised her a simple procedure after the regular blood tests, with no clinic stay. Yes, she could go right back home once it was done.

A shocked Jaya burst out, 'That's all? Is that all it takes?'

'Of course, darling, modern technology and lasers are very useful in cutting out blood, gore and painful recoveries. Just stay off sex for five days after the vaginal tightening procedure. By the way, who's the lucky guy?'

'This is more to make you feel whole, so I am just joking when I am saying this, yet…' broke in Mano.

So far, smooth sailing, with Mano bolstering her courage. By the end of the week, she was answering a call gaily.

'Hi Zenobia. Great hearing from you. How're all you, guys? Yes, I've recovered from that trip and a whole lot more too....'

'No worries, how's everyone else?'

'You say there is a bear with a sore head?' she giggled. 'Of course, you can tell him I miss him too.'

Three days later, the bell rang. Pushing her hair back with a smeared hand, she opened the door to RS! He gave her a quizzical smile as he put out his hand to wipe her forehead and envelop her in a bear hug. Finally, she held him off.

'I was just making something for tea. Interested in *bhajiyas*?'

'No.'

'No to hot fresh bhajiyas?'

'Not while you fry yourself in the kitchen? No thanks.'

'Join me,' she said as she led the way to cover one end of the platform with a clean towel to sit on. He made himself comfortable, his back to the fridge and feet up in front of him.

'No shoes on my platform,' Jaya swatted as she got busy with the bhajiyas.

'*Bolo*...?' Zenobia nudged her.

'Aren't your eyes and ears supposed to be closed?' she said to Zenobia and Sujit, RS's closest friends. She was smiling mischievously as she said that.

'Are you daft, Jaya? Such spicy revelations and we are supposed to keep a straight face?'

As she gathered her breath, bets were laid on 'Yes' and 'No' between the friends.

'The longer you hold back, the higher the stakes, Jaya,' RS admonished cheekily. She stuck her tongue out at him.

'For all the world, you are like a nine-year-old.'

'Add 50 to that,' Jaya countered. 'And keep guessing.'

Zenobia and Sujit made a strategic exit. RS put his hand gently on Jaya's.

'How often?' Pain flashed across her face.

'Every possible day, then zero for 14-odd years now.'

'Are all men here blind?' he asked.

'Look, see, but touch, no. None up to the mark.'

'So, I made your grade? Congrats to me?'

'You are talking about last night?' she, said, hesitatingly.

'A revelation that I need you in my life. You?'

'Finally, a firm pair of shoulders to lean on, strong arms for support,' she smiled. He leaned over to kiss the tip of her pert nose.

'Expecting a proposal?' he asked with a cynical smile. 'Usually, women do.'

'Am I the usual?' His face slid to one side as if considering what she had said.

'Not that I can judge.'

'Either way, NO!'

'Why?'

'You want to spoil a lovely morning?'

'That's exactly why I've toppled! Friends?'

'Friends.'
'And lovers.'
'Now that needs consideration.'
'What consideration?'
'Uff! Commitments. Too many....'
'Hubby's out. Kids?'

'Two *bahus*, grandkids and boys. Some of them are bindass, while some will nitpick. How do you manage?'

'I ignore them. Aren't I the original *bindass*, babe?'

'What do they have to do with your life?'

She sighed, 'I am Mom, Ma. They place me on a pedestal,' she said, scrunching up her nose.

'So don't say a word now. Later, let them learn to like it or lump it. Did they ask you before marrying?' She shook her head.

'You let them lead their own lives?' She nodded.

'Then ditto, you. Do we need the consent of pups?' he growled. 'How often do they look you up? Come to see Coorg. Why bake here, instead of catching its cool mists?'

Jaya wouldn't budge. There was work to do before ushering the summers in at home.

'Go, get some work done, one can't be on holiday all the time.'

An exhausting heatwave and the calls from the cool hills finally broke her resolve and Jaya headed out to the green hills, and their vista of calm verdancy. She loved the occasional dark patches, the innumerable streams tumbling down roadside channels. And the heavenly mists rolling across miles.

A fascinating variety of leafy ballets kept her eyes glued to the succession of solo ballets and group dances of the different trees en route, till exhaustion overtook her.

She recalled waking up in a canopied bed, looking out to a vision of misty hills. From her balcony, she spied a trim, lithe RS exercising; admiring his elegant greying at the temples, she shook her head at her own plump, salt-n-pepper self.

'What does RS stand for?'

'Rangaswamy, so RS.' Later, in the middle of another conversation, she said, 'I'm going to call you Ranga. Sounds sexier than RS.'

'Like in "Ranga Khush"?' smirked Sujit.

'No, Ranga as in the first half of his name.' There was no comeback on that one.

The next few days, there were endless conversations, in which they shared their troubled pasts, but their easy camaraderie made life no longer lonely, but abundant; a certain mental lightness in their demeanour made for cheery smiles that drew smirks and raised eyebrows from onlookers.

It was only natural to eventually move into Ranga's rooms with a boudoir of her own. Ranga's eyes twinkled, as he said, 'How does that matter now, Jaya? It happened for the better. Let's revel in it.'

After a couple of weeks, Zenobia remarked, 'Why don't you call your boys over for a break?'

Jaya frowned, 'Have a heart, Zen. My BP's normalising and you want to chase it back up?'

'That onerous, Jaya?' Ranga said, concerned.

'Let this be till I go back, rather than face a thousand questions.'

'Go back? For what? Loneliness? Playing Housie?'

'It's home. Festivals mean family time, and little ones come.'

'Wouldn't this be a more memorable holiday?' Her tremulous voice spoke her mind, that was repeating a pet phrase: 'Friends and lovers.'

Zenobia and Sujit quietly slipped away, leaving them alone.

'Is this so boring that you're ready to rush off in a few weeks?' he teased. 'Or is it a dilemma of acknowledgement?'

'Should I announce: "Come to Coorg, and meet my friend and lover?"'

'Let them come for a break, that coincides with their holidays and we'll ensure they have fun and adventure with grandma's Friend and Lover. Or else, marry me. Yours and mine are both in their own worlds, so why need anyone know? We'll remain F & L for everyone here. But we'll belong,' he said, pleading with his eyes, hands and lips.

Jaya remained apprehensive.

'Can't go through it all over again? Walking out and coming back, hiding emotions, battles, curses, bitterness, accusations....'

RS was shocked.

'Why would that happen? Why do you think it would be a repeat of an unhappy past? Talk reasonably. You really think I'd walk out on a woman like you?'

'RS, there are some basic facts to consider. Both of us are married, and neither is divorced. Different reasons, whatever. As legal entities, one day there will be unhappiness, stink, and whatnot. I can't handle all that. Sorry. Don't say 'no'. Your end maybe. But at my end, one kid letting one word drop and a tempest will blow. That's the way he's built, and there is no logic to it. He has a simple dog-in-the-manger mindset. Marriage cannot happen without a formal divorce and that will not happen. So let's be "Friends and Lovers". That's what we are. Why shift the balance?'

'I've no intention of making some pundit spouting vague mantras richer. I think it is just a marketing gimmick to collect *hafta* from shops, etc. Ever checked that out?' she said, raising an eyebrow. 'We're fine as we are now.'

'Jaya, a prayer never hurt anyone, did it? In a quiet temple, seeking the Lord's blessing for us, nobody else. That's it. Please don't be difficult and consider it.'

'Are you forever off on breaks like this?' she asked, eyes twinkling.

'Sujit can handle it. There're mobiles and email. I need time with you; let me look after you. I want you by my side always, doing all that you dream of but never do; I want to do that for my woman. Does that sound illegitimate?'

'You make it sound so easy, Ranga. Is it so?'

'What?' he frowned as she hesitated, opening and shutting her mouth, voicing her innermost fears.

'I was a one-man woman, but not 'woman enough' then. Woman enough now, more than a decade later? For you? For how long?'

He placed a finger on her lips and drew her close.

'Perish such thoughts. You just have to be your beautiful self. Let's just be happy pleasuring each other, for offering succour in a crisis, hurt or frustration, for just being there; sex is great; for the low spirit days....'

'Putting out your hand at night to find a soul to comfort you....'

'Exactly. What else? Your boys are there for whatever else you need.'

She rolled her eyes, 'I can just hear the chorus of 'MAAAAAs....'

'Why mortgage your happiness to your grownup, married kids? Let them take it on the chin—let them acknowledge that Mom was not made to be a nun.'

Weakening, the wise grandma enticed the grandkids, with tales of adventure camps, swimming in real streams and waterfalls, plus, special festivals, *Puttari* and *Kaveri*

Shankaramana, one which might possibly coincide with their Diwali break.

'Come see a new part of India, instead of travelling to some foreign country.'

To their elders, she sold the vista of silks, honey and coffee, with clubs and adventure thrown in.

They came, saw and were conquered in different ways: from the resort at a corner of the estate, the kids had their hearts' fill of open-air adventures, the boys revelled in both, the open-air adventures and the clubs, while the wives shopped till they dropped. Jaya was drained keeping up with it all. The festival loomed closer.

Towards the end of the Big Day, after the contests were over, when Jaya was escorted to the stage, the family's eyebrows rose as she gave away the awards, before lunch. An exhausted Jaya breathed heavily, watching the post-lunch festivities.

Zenobia signalled to RS who escorted her out into the garden. Her son, Amit followed the pair with his eyes, wondering.

'RS, take me back, please; it's too crowded to breathe.'

'Come home, Jaya,' he said, longingly. Exhaustion lined his face too.

'We're too tired. After they leave the day after, I'll be home and rest for a while.'

'Who'll I put out my hand to in the dark?'

She smiled tiredly, recalling her own dialogue.

RS and Sid, her other son, appeared. 'What's going on?' they asked.

Amit spoke out loud. Sid chose to be neutral.

'Let Ma enjoy herself once in a while, man. We've enjoyed this week here too, haven't we?'

'What if it's more than just enjoying?' Amit said, petulantly.

RS guided the conversation to where he wanted it to go.

'Let me tell all of you, that if your mother would only say 'Yes', I'd marry her tonight because there is immense love between us. But she can't take the possible ruckus that would ensue if we do. So, tell me, why are you sabotaging our genuine friendship? Do you genuinely want to leave her at the mercy of those catty crones and drakes that surround her back at that home? Believe me, I've been there and seen that. You were unfazed by that, but yet, here you are shitting bricks at a gentleman who cares?'

Amit's stand collapsed. The wives were delighted at the thought of an MIL out of sight, and Sid was quite sanguine to the idea. A 'family' brunch brought the visit to a close.

'Phew! Now I know why girls dread that first meeting with the in-laws!' His pals guffawed as RS wiped his forehead with a handkerchief.

Later, Sid's views were shared. He had said, 'Just please stick to Friends and Lovers. The day that second one ends, put Lovers aside and remain Friends. Not be at daggers drawn. No grand wedding. Only ensure my Ma's health and make hers a happier life.'

'Jaya, will you marry me without all the hoopla? Just you, me and a prayer?'

'RS, we both stand married already.'

'No one will know except probably Sid. It'll be just the two of us.'

Weeks of persuasion that it would not be a regular wedding—just a visit to a temple, and that's it, made Jaya relent. When shopping was suggested, Jaya raised her eyebrows.

'You only came kitted out for a ten-day trip. Let's go get some more, you'll need some things, at least.' Jaya looked at RS, wondering if Sid knew. He read her face, and smiled. 'Let's go shopping,' he said.

RS smiled indulgently. 'Go ahead, I know your yen for reds. But *the* sari is already being processed.'

'What about me?'

'My choice especially for my long-chased lady, who's way past middle age. Don't I deserve something, also?'

'Drop that hangdog look. Wasn't your choice of lady enough?' she said, as they both laughed.

'If I know you, you'll love it enough to wear it every day through the honeymoon too,' he said softly, eyes twinkled as he smiled.

'ACTUALLY?' SHE winked at Abha, the shopping assistant who was relieved at the no-tantrum throwing couple whom she was tending to. 'Can't tell how old folks react,' she thought to herself.

'Who says one couldn't fuck in a sari? Our ancestors did.'

'Want a trial run?' smirked RS.

'Thank you, I will pass that for now.'

'Then are you finished yet?'

'Please, sir, not even the silks, yet. Ma'am, red, which one?'

'Abha, find me a soft red one with a dramatic *pallu*, maybe maroon. Nothing stiff, please. And for the day stuff—a pastel colour, not a dead one; should be reasonably bright, floral if possible, but make it quick.'

'Coming up, but the silks?'

'Sweetie, a seven-day trip with that sari on all days? Do I need another silk for now? Find something please, one georgette or cotton, and yes, two skirts, one mid-calf and one ankle length; get two matching, simple, elegant tops for each, with comfy necks, sleeves, and loose at my boobs and bums. A nightie and a sarong, that's all I need. And yes Abha, find some earrings, neck or hands stuff and a beach bag, please.'

'With saris?'

'If that sari is on all the time, I'll need a bag, for sure.'

'Ma'am, give me 10 minutes and I'll show you some to select from,' Abha said, rushing out.

'*Uff, main marjawan. Eh ki kitta?*' (*This will* be the death of me, what have I done?)

'Jaya, what happened?' RS was by her side at once, concerned at the fatigue on her face.

'This,' she said, waving her arms, 'I am not even halfway, and tired of it, already.'

'Indulge me, love. You've never let me before.'

Abha walked in, wheeling in two racks. 'Please select, Ma'am,' she said.

'To match with what, Abha? Wrong order of stuff!' she said, giggling over the rack of accessories.

'You may like something and match the garment with the bag or a bangle. Could happen.'

RS egged her on. Eventually, some shopping happened. Then the Big Day dawned.

A blindfold cut off her vision after her face and hair were done. She felt incredibly soft silk being draped around her. Goose bumps gleamed on her bare skin. She caressed the fabric gently.

He held her close, all through the trek in the hills surrounded by the dawn, peace and tranquility. After a prayer, they descended, then approached the sea.

'I can smell the sea, even hear some.'

Soon enough, she was being guided to their suite. Senses acute, she heard RS's steps, a barefoot approach as he dropped a kiss on her forehead. Then light seemed to flood in; the blindfold was gone and her eyes protested at the sudden flash. Slowly, they focused on the mirror's vision glowing in a luscious red, with silver mauve border 'n' pallu.

'Worth the wait?' he asked. She smiled up at him in the mirror.

'Luscious! You knew I'd never say no to this.'

'Seven days?'

'You'll get bored,' she said, wrinkling her nose at him. But he wanted just that. Every morning, the sari waited for her, freshly aired and ironed; indulgent smiles and curious glances from fellow guests followed the silver-haired couple who were so lost in their own world, jibber-jabbering amidst the lush green of the Kerala coast, its palms and its beaches.

One morning, they took a boat ride. As she stepped into the little craft, a protruding nail snagged at the sari, leaving a long tear. Jaya was aghast, and RS more so, concerned over her copious weeping.

'Our utterly divine sari's now torn. Life's always so unfair,' she railed, sobbing into his shoulder. He signalled the push-off, but Jaya was inconsolable. Like all older women, she had her fixations—he had gotten the sari for forever, and it was now defiled by the long tear. It cast a shadow on their tryst with the cradling waves and the seagulls riding the minuscule peaks, oblivious to anything but their swinging, perhaps.

That night, she took it off and folded it neatly,

shedding tears as she set it aside. He never knew when she got up in the wee hours and spread the sari over the waters rushing out with the tide, whispering, 'Go into good hands, my sari. *Rab Raakhe* (God keep you).'

It was RS's turn to be horrified, now. And then, furious. 'How could you, Jaya? You actually let the sari into the tide? How could you do that to my sari for you?'

'And hold you up to insult, wearing a damaged piece? How I wish I had worn the skirt instead. Keeping the torn sari would be a constant reminder. So, I let the tide decide its fate. Don't the gods decide? Now let the Tide God decide the sari's fate.'

Much later, she apologised for letting her fancies get the better of her; she was even properly remorseful, pleading, but finally, she lost her temper.

'You listen to me, RS', she said, wagging a finger at his nose, 'We decided to never let communication suffer. And you're sulking. This is not what you promised me. And all this for a sari?'

RS gave up with a groan.

'Oh Jaya, I wanted to see you in that sari forever. How could you let it go like that?'

That night, there was extraordinary desperation in their lovemaking as if both were making up for lost time and apologising to each other and to themselves.

As usual, RS rose early to step out for his dawntime walk, his face morose. As he walked, his eyes were on the sea, looking for that ray of colour on the water lightening up as dawn peeped, hoping the tide would somehow bring it back.

His eyes slid over the beach ahead, and he saw a man running towards him, arms folded across his chest. Curious, he continued to gaze at the strange running posture, till the man waved. Panting, he reached RS, holding out a green palm leaf package that he had held close to his chest.

'Saar, Madame's. It came back to our village,' he said, gesturing behind him. Hope, anger, love, and frustration chased across RS's face as he opened the package …. Yes, it was the red sari! Neatly washed and ironed, as good as new despite its sea bath.

'Saar, my mother repaired it. The neighbour said Madame wears it every day, so I brought it. She must wear it today also, no? Couldn't get a new one. So sorry, our boys don't maintain boats.' The poor man was reduced to silence by the wonder on the other man's face as his fingers skimmed over the luscious silk, softer than before. After a futile attempt at a reward, RS clasped the man's shoulders in thanks and jogged back, wondering how to break the news to Jaya.

He knew she was awake but unmoving as he slid into the room. Gently spreading it over her, he bent to kiss her forehead, whispering, 'Good morning, Love.' Her eyes shot open, looking into his in wonder, pearls dammed at the rims.

'RS, you're back!' she said, clutching him desperately. He noted the desperation, and pointed down; she looked, unable to believe what she saw, the red sari over her nakedness. Almost automatically, her fingers flew to caress the soft supple fabric as she looked into his eyes.

'It's come back to us, RS? Where did you find it?' she asked, even as he sealed her lips with a kiss and a demand, 'Promise you'll never, never let it go, again.' He held out his hand to cover hers. RS examined her face, the plump cheeks still pale, those intelligent eyes sorrowful, her soft hands flapping and the breath coming heavy. She was startlingly unpretentious, and now her unmade-up face was almost in tears.

'Jaya,' he said, putting his hands gently on her shoulders, then, rubbing gently down her back, 'Hasn't the Tide God returned your sari to us?' he asked, smiling.

For once she was lost for words to express her emotions.

'What do I say? The thought frightens me.' She shivered delicately, unable to either hide her feelings or express it. RS took hold of the fluttering hands and soothed them.

'Jaya, there will always be varied reactions to different situations. This morning, when I woke you with the sari, you were desperate because you thought I'd left you, weren't you?' he said, while looking straight into her eyes. When her eyelids dipped, he gave her a hug.

'See how foolish, thoughts can be? Never ever again

compare yourself to any material object. You know you are Jaya, too, don't you?' ('Jaya' means 'victory' in Hindu philosophy.)

They clung to each other desperately, making up for the lost night.

A New Dimension, Perhaps?

Mr and Mrs Dhupia were inconsolable.

Their daughter had gone and got married! Moved out of their upmarket, picture-perfect, spacious apartment into his pad. Now transforming it into a home was a full-time task—and she had no time for homesickness.

At a get together, silver-haired Mrs Dhupia held forth:

'The house feels so cold, empty, huge. Just the two of us rattling around in all those empty rooms. Why couldn't he have moved in? There is plenty of space for all of us.'

Her *samdhan* Aarti, the mother of the maligned groom, seemed cold, hard and unfeeling.

'I've been down that road...when each of our boys moved out of our huge mansion which too has plenty of room for all. Young people love their independence. Instead of that giving in to that Empty Nest Syndrome,

But they were ambushed by the boys. Jaya pleaded exhaustion till RS cut in firmly, saying, 'She needs to rest now. Can't it wait for a few hours?'

Amit was furious. 'Who is this guy who's all over you, Ma?'

She put her hand on his arm, saying, 'Is liking my company a crime?'

'If you're not well, we'll look after you.'

Jaya sat up straight.

'When did you last see me before this, any of you?' she looked around at the group. 'Six months, nine months ago? Not disturbing your lives should mean no friends for me? What's your problem?'

One of the wives said, 'You're Ma.'

'*Matlab*, I live like a nun with no one to bother about me? In health or illness? Yesterday, it was Zenobia who noticed me breathing heavily and told RS. None of you noticed that I was tired.'

'You didn't tell us. But he does behave almost like a lover.'

'So? What about it?'

'Ma? Of course, it matters!' the *bahus* were strident.

'So, if someone cares enough about me as a person to look out for me if I enjoy myself holidaying with friends, it troubles you? What's the problem?'

'Ma...Dad!'

'What does he have to do with this? When did you last see him?'

try rejuvenating your lives to become comfortable and lead your own lives now.'

'You're so unfeeling,' shuddered Mrs Dhupia.

'What's 'unfeeling' about it? They want their own life. Didn't you? So, give the same right to them.'

'But he takes up all her time....'

'Yes... Come to think of that, maybe you'll now have more sympathy for your mother-in-law than you've ever had before.' Mrs Dhupia glared at her, furiously. A loud cackle of laughter erupted from behind her.

The older Mrs Dhupia senior looked up from her hand of cards.

'Forget it. That is one thing that will never happen in this lifetime.'

Aarti looked up with questioning eyes taking in the closed faces in front of her as well as Mr Dhupia's helpless look.

'No go, I guess. Just thought that since your mother obviously came to terms with her loss ages ago, perhaps it could have given a new dimension to your relationship; given it some meaning, you know. But then, perhaps not?'

Musings Through My Bedroom Window

Through my bedroom window, I look down at a giant bedroom.

It can sleep 23-odd, scattered around in singles, doubles, triples and more.

The dark nights offer no glimpse of those that I rush to catch at daylight.

My eyes first seek out the horizon, shuttered by rising skyscrapers. Monster steel and glass developments that slurp resources spew out fake humans with phoney emotions that change with every audience:

Ultra-right/left, MOD/outdated, liberal/conservative, 50/50....

They give fulsome praise to your face, yet offer vicious criticism behind your back.

Much before the skyscrapers are swathes of variegated greens, the trees swaying majestically in the early morning breeze. It's easy to pick out those trees with a new coat. They come in fresh new shades of glistening green, standing out from the mature shades around them of the older trees.

Then the eyes reach closer home, focussing on the terrace immediately below my eyrie. There, just below my window, is an old thick-set man on his solitary string bed with two pillows, positioned to allow him to sleep until a little late, under the shadow of the overhang of the adjoining room that screens off the earliest sunrays. On occasions, a young grandson joins him on a smaller bed close by. Three other family members sleep well away from the old man, rising early to quietly move off, without disturbing the patriarch.

Those who sleep on the northeastern corner of the terrace, diagonally opposite, are not so lucky. The first rays of the sun strike full in the face of whoever sleeps there– and only a young lazy boy covers his face, as if challenging the rays to get through. That battle earns him the dubious honour of having to fold all the bedclothes, stack all the beds against the wall and the bedclothes on the beds.

On the northwest of the terrace, across from where the old man slumbers, a foursome of beds is cooled by a handsome pedestal fan. Often, I imagine them squabbling over the placement of the beds in the lee of the stairwell that offers some shade from the sun's first rays. One whole bed is so shielded that if offers an extra 10 minutes of sleep before the harsh sunlight bores into the eyes.

One morning I was late! Only the last bed on that western corner was occupied by the time I reached the window. A middle-aged woman had come up gracefully up the stairs and was surveying the terrace, now bereft of sleepers, except for our lone sleepyhead. Why do women never sleep late, I asked myself.

Her hair and sari were so perfectly in order, that I guessed that she must have already done tea, prepared the family breakfast and had a little wash before heading back up. With practised ease, she picked up her bed and placed it horizontally against the adjoining wall that offered her family some privacy from the other segment of the terrace and offered the longest shaded lee against the heat. As she moved each bed, the bedcovers went onto the adjacent one, till they were all piled onto the recalcitrant sleeper who was thus forced to sit up. With incredible grace and patience, the lady folded each just so, then neatly piled them up on the stacked beds. Finally, the boy got up, gathered all the pillows and marched off with them, downstairs, while the mother stood up the last bed and covered the whole lot with an old black cover. Then with one hand, she picked up the pedestal fan to stand it in a shaded corner, covering it too, before sweeping off downstairs.

Now, only one little corner of the terrace stood empty of the outdoor sleepers, a little enclosed space with doors firmly shut. Four pairs of big and small slippers outside revealed the strength inside.

Looking down onto the now empty terrace, I thought the morning had come into the house from my upstairs window. In that instant, loud sounds of jubilation rose. Were they from the ground floor, from an area that I had never seen? The middle-floor flats had protruding balconies which were their summer bedrooms. After a while, loud wails took over. I wondered what was happening to my people.

My people? I didn't know any of them from Adam. To tell the truth, I had never even seen their faces properly with my rheumy eyes from so afar. Yet they were mine! They had been my early morning companions for so many years now.

The dhobi's brother arrived to pick up the day's ironing after a half hour's impatient wait. 'Where's your brother?' I asked him.

'His daughter scored above 90 per cent in the Board results. They've gone to the school,' he announced with great pride. 'Tonight, we will celebrate after work.'

'But I could hear some people crying, too. What happened?'

'A call came from the village. Bhabhi's mother died and she's gone to the village.'

The good and the bad–both happening on the same day among our people. Doesn't that happen, everywhere?

★ ★ ★